VAN DYNE'S VAMPIRES

PIERCE MOSTYN PARANORMAL INVESTIGATIONS
BOOK 4

C W HAWES

This one's for Susannah

ENTER THE IMAGINATIVE WORLD OF CW HAWES

Enter my world. A world of terror on a cosmic scale. Just click, tap, or scan the QR code below.

Fear is the most primal of human emotions. And fear of the unknown is the most terrifying of all fears.

If you are new to the Pierce Mostyn Paranormal Investigations series, then *Terror in the Shadows* is an excellent entry point into the series and into my world.

In addition to my Pierce Mostyn Paranormal Investigations books, I've written short stories set in the world of the macabre and arcane. Many of which are only available to folks on my mailing list.

So just click, tap, or scan the QR code to enter my world of terror and the macabre. You will get a free copy of *The Feeder* and you'll get my monthly email of news and curated contact. Terror awaits!

1

THE MOON WAS HIDDEN behind the clouds. However, the parking lot and the grounds surrounding the building were bathed in yellow light from the high-pressure sodium lamps.

Hunkered down in a grove of trees some distance away from the lot was Special Agent in Charge Pierce Mostyn, who studied the brightly lit area with his binoculars. Next to him was Special Agent Kymbra NicAskill, a new recruit for the Office of Unidentified Phenomena. She also had a pair of binoculars and was studying the building and surrounding area. Both were dressed in black jumpsuits.

"What do you see, NicAskill?"

"A lot of lights and a lot of security cameras. You, sir?"

"The same." Mostyn set his binoculars aside.

"The lights and cameras will make it difficult to reach the building undetected."

Mostyn cast a sideways glance at NicAskill. Another recruit. He didn't know how Bardon found them. However, he couldn't help but think that sooner or later Bardon would run out of prospects. Lately, the OUP had suffered a higher than average attrition rate. The cosmic forces had been especially difficult and the agents too green. Unseasoned cannon fodder.

NicAskill was an attractive woman. Difficult to see that through her battle dress. But in a skirt, blouse, and jacket, as he'd seen her the first time, she'd turn any man's head. So why in God's name was she with the OUP?

He let out a sigh.

"Sir?"

"Nothing, NicAskill. The lights and cameras will be a problem, but the bigger problem will be the security personnel and the dogs. That's why we have Bardon's Folly along."

"Do you think it will work, sir?"

"Probably work as well as any of the other OUP issued toys we get."

"Probably?"

Mostyn shrugged. "Okay. Definitely."

"You aren't helping things, sir."

"Haven't you ever flown before?"

"Not in a two-person blimp."

"Up until a week ago I hadn't either. And here I am to talk about it. C'mon, NicAskill. Time to get airborne."

Rising off a grassy field ten miles away from the Van Dyne Corporation building was a black shadowy shape. SNOB 1. Mostyn loved the acronym for the Special Night Operations Blimp. He thought it fitting for what he called Bardon's Folly. Dr. Rafe Bardon was the director of the OUP, one of the most secret of the government's secret agencies.

One hundred twelve feet long and twenty-eight feet wide at its widest point, SNOB 1 was a two-man personal blimp the OUP had modified for special operational use. Powered by an electric motor for silent operation, it could be radio-controlled in the event the craft became crewless.

The most novel part of the small airship was that it was inflated with a rare form of hydrogen, H_3, to give it greater lift. Just slightly heavier than normal hydrogen, H_3 is not flammable when mixed with air. If the gas wasn't so expensive to produce, it just might revolutionize air travel.

Mostyn piloted the silent craft across the New Jersey countryside, maintaining an altitude of fifteen hundred feet. NicAskill, meanwhile, double-checked their equipment.

"Don't you think we're going in somewhat lightly armed, sir?"

"What do you want, NicAskill, a howitzer? We have those thermite incendiary charges to lug down to the eighth and ninth floors. How much more stuff do you want to carry?"

"I understand, sir. But we'll be facing a small army of security people once we're in the building."

"I wouldn't be too worried about the *people*. It's the other things we might find in there that I'm concerned about."

"That's what I mean, sir. A pistol, combat utility knife, stun and smoke grenades, and the portable lightning generator. That's not much, sir."

"You've trained on the M-88, right?"

"Yes, sir. It's an awesome weapon, but a bit slow for combat situations. I mean, fifteen seconds to recharge?"

Mostyn grinned. "If there's anything left to recharge for."

"Still..."

Mostyn held up his hand. "Sumer Base, we are one minute to target. Do you read me?"

"We read you, Mostyn. There's a problem on our end."

"What kind of problem, Langstor?"

"Riley, here, Mostyn. They changed security codes on me.

I'm doing my best to get in so we can fudge the security cameras for you."

Mostyn's face showed concern. "Do you think they know we're coming?"

"No, I don't think so," Riley said. "I think they just ran a routine change."

"Let's hope you're right, Riley," Mostyn replied.

Langston's voice came on. "If Riley can't find a way into their system, we'll abort."

"Roger," Mostyn replied. "We are in position in five, four, three, two, one, now."

Mostyn turned the airship into the faint wind coming out of the south and set the engines to provide enough prop rotation to hold position.

"Sumer Base are you ready to take control of the blimp?" he asked.

"Not yet," Langston said.

"C'mon, Riley," Mostyn muttered.

"Okay, I'm in," Riley said. "Now give me half a minute." There was a pause, and then, "Okay, the code's inserted. The cameras will read the pixels in your clothing and interpret the data as nothing. They won't see you."

Langston's voice came back on. "Sumer Base is taking control of your blimp. Now get down there and destroy some mutants."

"Roger that," Mostyn replied.

There was a frown on NicAskill's face. "Sir, I signed up to help defend the United States, but I don't understand why we are attacking Americans."

"To be honest, NicAskill, this entire operation is a bit sketchy. Bardon didn't provide a lot of background. From what he did provide and what I discovered doing a bit of snooping, van Dyne is connected to some pretty powerful groups.

Groups that often function as shadow governments. The thought is that whatever he's creating in his labs is going to be used to destabilize legitimate governments to allow all sorts of thugs to take over."

"Like the Mafia running the world?"

"Something like that. Now cut the questions and let's go."

The two OUP agents donned their bulletproof vests and equipment harnesses. NicAskill had already lowered the lines while Mostyn was talking with Sumer Base. They attached their descenders to the lines and abseiled the three hundred feet from the blimp to the roof of the Van Dyne building.

The summer night air was warm and slightly moist. The sky was overcast. All was quiet on the roof. Mostyn watched the lines retract into the blimp, and then the airship slowly motored off into the night.

"Kind of bright up here, sir. We might not register on the cameras, but do you think our shadows will?"

"Quit worrying, NicAskill, and find the door so we can get inside."

The roof was covered with asphalt, and mostly flat. On the south end was a structure that looked like three or four very large cardboard boxes thrown together. On the north end was a slightly raised rectangle. Surrounding the roof was a three-foot high wall.

Mostyn pointed at the rectangle. "That will be the emergency exit from the rear stairwell. No outside access." He pointed towards the cuboid structure and indicated NicAskill should follow him. He crouched next to the low wall and proceeded towards the structure.

He was glad the wall was there. Not fond of heights, he wouldn't want to creep along the roof edge with nothing between him and the ground below.

They were fifty feet from the structure, when a large dark

shape rounded a corner and rushed them. Even though Mostyn was in the lead, it was NicAskill who fired the three double-taps from her silenced pistol that finally dropped the thing.

"What the hell is that, sir?"

"Looks to me like pictures of Cerberus."

"What?"

"Cerberus. Greek mythology. The three-headed dog that stopped the dead from leaving Hades. And probably anyone alive from entering."

"My God, the thing's huge."

"Yeah. Must be at least three hundred pounds."

"And three heads."

Mostyn pointed. "I think that's the entrance point we're looking for. And NicAskill?"

"Sir?"

"Welcome to Hell."

The look on her face showed she wasn't too keen on the visit.

They walked over to the door, which was illuminated by a low-watt bulb.

"You have your contact in, right?"

"I do, sir."

She keyed in the security code and let the retina scanner scan her right eye. There was a click, the light on the keypad changed from red to green, and NicAskill pulled the door open.

Mostyn entered and pulled his night vision goggles over his eyes. In a soft voice he spoke into the mouthpiece of his headset. "We are in, Sumer Base. Activating body cam now."

Langston replied, "Any trouble?"

"Minor. They're breeding three hundred pound dogs with three heads. NicAskill just took one out."

"Just the one?"

"So far."

Mostyn slowly descended the stairwell, which was illuminated by a few small globes that cast a greenish light. The walls appeared to be made of cinder blocks and were painted what Mostyn thought was probably an off-white, although the illumination made them look green. Behind him he heard NicAskill attach the stock and strap to the TACLIG M-88, the Tactical Lightning Generator.

The M-88 looked similar to the old Mauser C-96 semiautomatic pistol. However, rather than shoot bullets, the M-88 shot a bolt of lightning. Making the small weapon very destructive. On the downside, the weapon was heavy for its size, slow to recharge, and there was the loud sonic boom accompanying the lightning bolt.

They reached a landing. Next to the door was a placard with the number 15 on it. Mostyn pointed to it and signaled they'd continue their descent.

He thought it odd the stairwell was so dimly lit, and try as he might he was unable to come up with an explanation that made sense. What he knew for certain was that it didn't seem normal, and he didn't like what wasn't normal.

Then again, in his line of work, Mostyn rarely came across what could be called "normal". Take that three-headed dog, for instance.

When they'd reached the tenth floor, Mostyn turned to NicAskill. "I don't like this. It's been too easy."

"I was thinking the same thing, sir."

"Keep your eyes peeled. We'll go down to eight, plant the charge, go back up to nine and plant the charge there. Then we get out of here."

"Right, sir."

"Sumer Base, you copy?"

"We copy, Mostyn," Langston said. "The blimp will be waiting for you."

"Acknowledged, Sumer Base."

Mostyn signaled to NicAskill to follow him and down the stairs they went, passing Level 9 and going on to the eighth floor.

"Okay, NicAskill, do your thing."

She typed in the security code and let the retina scanner scan her right eye. There was a click, and the light on the keypad moved from red to green.

NicAskill slowly pushed the door open. In a moment they were looking at a large room filled with tables, glass cabinets, and shelves. The lighting was dim. Scattered nightlights near the floor provided the only illumination. It was, however, sufficient for Mostyn's and NicAskill's night vision goggles and they were able to see the room clearly.

"What's that in the center, sir?"

"Looks like an operating theater."

"They create those three-headed dogs here?"

"Probably do the initial whatever, then move them up to nine. Come on. Let's plant the charge and get out of here."

"But what's the point, sir? I guess I'm still in the dark as to why we're here."

"We just follow orders. Remember?"

"Yes, sir."

"But to answer your question, I don't know exactly. There's that sketchy intel that van Dyne wants to sell his monsters to third world dictators, liberation army leaders, mobsters, anyone looking for an instrument of terror. In my instructions for this mission, Bardon didn't say much. He intimated Van Dyne Corp is possibly intending to use these creatures to create situations of wide spread panic, allowing the thugs of the world to then take advantage of the resulting chaos. Which could possibly lead to the overthrow of the world's legitimate governments, with a possible take over by van Dyne. However, it's all really rather sketchy at this point. So who knows?"

"Why are we here then, if nobody really knows what's going on?"

"Think of it as a preemptive strike. After all, you don't want to come home from work one day and see your neighbor with a three-headed dog, do you?"

She digested that for a moment, noticed Mostyn's smile, and nodded.

Mostyn heard Langston say, "Your body cam sensor is picking up a heat signature to your right. In that little ell.

Mostyn gave NicAskill the hand signal that they had company and pointed in the general direction, just in case Langston's voice hadn't come through.

Langston's voice again. "Looks like one of those three-headed dogs from the heat outline."

"Great," Mostyn whispered back.

In his ear he heard, "We've patched the heat image through to your goggles so the two of you can see the thing."

"Thanks," Mostyn replied. After a moment he said, "Ah, there it is. Right in that ell, hidden from view."

NicAskill whispered, "It's just hunkered down in the corner. Looks like it's listening to us. Funny it hasn't attacked."

"Maybe three heads aren't better than one. Give me your backpack. You watch that thing, while I set the charge."

She slipped out of the backpack and handed it to Mostyn.

"It's getting up, sir."

"Keep your eye on it, and shoot if you have to."

Mostyn started making his way across the room, when the Cerberus creature came around the corner; all three throats emitting a low-pitched growl. Mostyn set the backpack down and took his pistol from its holster. He flipped off the safety and pulled the hammer back.

The beast crouch down and then ran towards Mostyn. Both he and NicAskill fired their silenced weapons at the thing, seemingly without effect. The huge three-headed canine leaped into the air. Mostyn dropped to the floor, rolled onto his back, and continued firing at the thing as it sailed over him.

The creature hit the floor with a soft thud, slid, and crashed into a glass cabinet, which set off an alarm.

NicAskill ran up to Mostyn. "Are you okay, sir?"

"I'm fine." He got up. "We need to get out of here."

In his ear, Mostyn heard Langston's voice saying the word, "Abort!"

"Do any of these tables move?" Mostyn asked NicAskill.

"Don't know, sir."

Mostyn grabbed the backpack and set it against a row of glass cabinets. He opened a pocket, and pressed a button on the device.

"Okay, time to get the hell out of here," he said.

In Mostyn's ear Langston was repeating the order to abort the mission. Mostyn said nothing in reply and ran towards the door by which he and NicAskill had entered the room, she running with him.

Before they got there, it slammed open and four guards stepped into the room, their helmet-mounted lights and rifle-mounted lasers sweeping the area before them.

Caught in the lights, Mostyn and NicAskill ducked just in time to miss being the recipients of four streams of automatic weapons fire. A big boxy tabletop with drawers and cabinets underneath, provided cover.

Mostyn tossed a stun grenade at them and the flash-bang gave the OUP agents momentary relief. As they got up to leave, a second contingent of security personnel stormed into the room. And once again, Mostyn and NicAskill ducked to avoid unwanted lead contamination.

NicAskill raised the M-88 so the barrel was just over the tabletop and pulled the trigger. There was a brilliant flash of light, like a hundred suns had just appeared in the room, and a thunder boom that shook the floor and shattered glass.

Mostyn's tactical earplugs muted the boom to a dull thud. He slowly stood up. The doorway and half the wall was one great big gaping hole.

He waved his arm. "Let's go!"

NicAskill followed him to the stairwell. The security personnel that hadn't been vaporized, showed severe burns and shrapnel damage from flying pieces of the exploding wall. Sprawled out on the stairs going down, there was an odd looking creature.

"Look at that, sir. Reminds me of the ogres I've seen in video games."

"It sure as hell ain't Shrek. C'mon." Mostyn started up the stairs, paused, looked back at NicAskill and said, "Video games?"

"Yes, sir."

He shook his head, and ran up the stairs. Muzzle flashes and pinging bullets indicated a security detail was coming up the stairwell behind them. On the landing for the ninth floor, Mostyn stopped, took off his backpack and opened the top. He reset the timer, pressed the activation button, and heaved the thing over the stair railing. A bullet grazed his vest, and knocked him down.

The incendiary explosion shot flames up the center of the stairwell. NicAskill helped Mostyn to his feet, then opened the door to the room on the ninth floor, and pulled the trigger on the M-88. The lightning bolt melted glass and steel and the thunder boom blew out the windows. Moments later the thermite bomb on the eighth floor exploded, the stairwell momentarily illuminated in the brilliant flash of light.

"Are you all right, sir?"

"I'm fine, Kymbra, let's go."

Up the stairs they ran, and burst out onto the roof. They paused a moment to catch their breath, and that's when they saw them.

"Looks like we got company, sir."

"I see that."

The two agents hit the hard surface of the roof as the three two-headed ogre-like beings opened fire with their machine guns. Bullets ricocheted off the cuboid structure, and smacked into the asphalt around them.

There was a pause as the mutant creatures reloaded. Mostyn and NicAskill where up, firing their silenced pistols. One of the things went down, the others returned fire sending Mostyn and NicAskill back to hugging the asphalt.

Mostyn heard Langston say, "The cavalry in four, three, two, one."

Fifty-caliber machine gun fire rent the night. SNOB-1, bow angled down, was a hundred feet above the building. Bullets showered the roof and the ogre things fell in a heap, blood and fragments of bone spraying out over the roof.

Mostyn and NicAskill were up and running to the abseil lines hanging from the blimp's gondola.

From out of the north emergency entrance came a small army of things that hell would refuse entrance.

The two agents grabbed the lines, and they heard Langston's voice say, "Hold on!"

Ballast dropped from the blimp and soaked the two agents. The propellers started spinning faster and the blimp made a sharp turn, flying away from the building, and into the New Jersey night.

2

TWO MONTHS LATER

THE PHONE in Mostyn's pocket was ringing. He rolled the creeper out from under the Columbia Six and fished the thing out of his pocket.

"Mostyn."

Helene Dubreuil rolled her creeper out from under the car and looked with wide-eyed wonderment at the oil coating her finger. After a moment, she stuck her finger in her mouth at the same time Mostyn yelled, "Don't!"

Then to the phone, he said, "No, not you, sir."

He heard a chuckle on the other end of the line. "Helene must be with you."

"Ooh, Mostyn Pierce, what a new experience!"

Dr. Rafe Bardon's burst of laughter caused Mostyn to hold the phone away from his ear.

"What is she experiencing now?"

"Motor oil," Mostyn said. "I swear, she's like a kid. Sticks everything in her mouth."

"Ah, that's what my sister always said about her children."

Huh, Mostyn thought, *never knew Bardon had family. Wonders never cease.*

Bardon continued, "I have a case for you. Come in as soon as possible. Helene, too."

"Yes, sir."

After a pause, Bardon said, "Motor oil isn't good for you, is it?"

"No, sir. No need to worry. She just licked a little off her finger."

"Oh, good. Well, then, goodbye."

Mostyn put the phone back in his pocket. To Helene he said, "Bardon. We have a case. He wants us ASAP."

She turned to him. "Oh, good, more new experiences! Mostyn Pierce, I'm so glad I came to your world." She hugged him and kissed him. "I feel so, so *alive!*"

Mostyn looked at the tall, pale-skinned, and dark-haired woman next to him, and smiled. She was literally out of this world. For Helene Dubreuil, the former H'tha-dub, was from the subterranean world of K'n-yan. She was human, but not *homo sapiens*. Her people having come to earth with the Great Old Ones eons ago.

He touched her face. So beautiful. She jumped up and extended her hand to him. He took it and pulled her back down to him.

"Oh, Mostyn Pierce, are you going to make Dr. Bardon wait?"

"He said as soon as possible, not immediately."

"You are a devil, Mostyn Pierce." She pressed her lips to his, and there was no more talking.

———

Dr. Rafe Bardon sat behind his large and heavy black walnut desk. His office was decorated in nineteenth century British men's club, which suited him and his British accent. He puffed on his pipe. The air smelled of sweet Virginia tobacco.

Across from him sat Mostyn and Helene. They were listening to the OUP director's telling of the legend of the Jersey Devil.

"Legend is always based on some nugget of fact, a tiny truth, which grows with the telling and eventually takes on a life of its own. And so a dislike of the Leeds family produced Leeds Devil, which eventually became the infamous Jersey Devil."

He paused for a moment to tamp the tobacco in his pipe, then continued."An odd looking creature. Supposedly having the head of a goat, bat-like wings, small arms with claws for hands, cloven hooves for feet, and a forked tail. And I might add that it goes without saying the creature moves very quickly and emits a blood-curdling scream."

"There is a creature similar to this in K'n-yan," Helene said.

Bardon looked surprised, and he hardly ever did so. "Really, Helene?"

She nodded.

"Very interesting. Perhaps..." Bardon sat for a moment, hands folded on his desk, face cast upwards. To Mostyn he had the look of a person pondering something. Then the director leaned back in his chair and continued.

"Of more recent origin and having a wider geographical distribution is the legend of the chupacabra. The notorious "goat-sucker", first sighted in Puerto Rico in nineteen ninety-five. Since then sightings have occurred as far north as Maine and as far south as Chile. With additional sightings in Russia and the Philippines."

"What does this thing look like, sir?" Mostyn asked.

"Supposedly it is a heavy creature, about the size of a small bear, with a row of spines along its back."

"Is it an alien?" Mostyn replied.

"Something that is not naturally occurring on this planet? Something that is from off world?" Bardon asked.

Mostyn nodded.

"Possibly. Possibly. I'm inclined not to think so, however, because nineteen ninety-five is three years after we learned of Van Dyne Corporation's experiments. Then, again, it might be a rare coincidence."

Mostyn shrugged.

"Precisely. Your mission is to determine what's behind the current rash of sightings."

"I haven't heard of any sightings," Mostyn said.

Helene was all smiles and filled with an excitement that reminded him of a child in a toy store. "That is because you do not spend time on the internet, my dearest. I learn so much of this world and I never have to leave the house."

Bardon smiled. "Very true."

Helene went on. "The earth is flat and it is a ball. There is a woman in New York who weighs two thousand pounds and hasn't moved in ten years. All the glaciers are melting and the next Ice Age is going to happen very soon. In fact, we are overdue for it. In K'n-yan our water never froze. I did not know it could do such a thing!"

Mostyn touched her hand. "The chupacabra?"

"Yes, yes. The goat-sucker creature. I have seen reports on dailymeteor.co.uk, the dazzle.com, foxnews.com, and YouTube. It has been seen in Belarus, North Carolina, western Texas, New Mexico, Arizona, and New Jersey. All in the past three years."

Bardon's eyes twinkled. "Very good, Helene. I had best be careful. You might be taking over my job one of these days."

"Oh, no, sir. Never!"

Bardon slid a folder across his desk towards Mostyn, who leaned forward in his chair and retrieved it.

"The sightings on the Arizona and New Mexico border, those in North Carolina, and also New Jersey appear to have the most validity, so start there," Bardon said. "You'll meet your other team members at the Osage tonight. I'll let you decide how to proceed from there."

"Thank you, sir," Mostyn said.

Bardon stood. "A pleasure seeing you again, Helene. And you, as well, Pierce. Good luck."

On the way out of the building, Mostyn paged through the folder and found the list of team members. There, at the top of the list, was Dr. Dotty Kemper.

Mostyn groaned and wondered what on earth Bardon was thinking.

3

IN A SMALL MEETING room at the Osage Hotel, Mostyn looked over the group of people assigned to him for this mission.

He knew Willie Lee Baker, their photographer, and special agent DC Jones, from previous missions. He also knew Dr. Dotty Kemper, perhaps the top forensic anthropologist on the planet, and OUP consultant Helene Dubreuil, because he was in an odd polyamorous relationship with the two women. A relationship he suspected of having been engineered by Dr. Bardon to keep his "best" people available for missions.

The three he didn't know had a long history with the OUP, and Mostyn found that comforting. No newbies on this mission.

Dr. Roderick Gerstner was a mythologist and one of Bardon's "go to" persons. He was forty-seven, six feet tall, and wore glasses. He and his wife, Connie, had three children.

Dr. Anthony Penn was a forensic veterinarian, and one of the best in the field. He was thirty-nine, six-one, wore glasses, and was built like a boxcar. He had a wife and two children.

Agent Carter Ramsey was a tech genius and was along to help with specialized surveillance.

Mostyn greeted the men and introduced them to the other team members. When introductions were completed, Mostyn addressed the team.

"After looking over the material Dr. Bardon has provided, I've decided we'll start our investigation in the southwest."

Dr. Gerstner interrupted. "Why there? Why not in New Jersey or North Carolina? After all, they're closer."

Dotty Kemper answered. "Because, Rod, he's saving the best for last. That's how Mostyn works."

A frown descended on Gerstner's face, but he didn't say anything. Mostyn continued.

"What we know about the latest appearances and attacks of the chupacabra is that outwardly they conform to previous reports. What is different this time is that we have surveillance camera verification of a sizable creature attacking and draining the blood of sheep and cattle. We've also secured two sheep carcasses and a cow carcass which Dr. Penn has been able to examine. What can you tell us, Dr. Penn?"

Anthony Penn leaned back in his chair. He had an almost bored expression on his face. Mostyn couldn't tell if he was truly bored or just happened to look that way.

Penn said, "The animals had been physically attacked and manhandled. It appears they were actually held down while the blood was taken, which implies the chupacabra has great strength. There was a single wound at the throat: a circular bruise with four puncture marks. The animals I examined had lost over ninety-five percent of their blood."

"How long had they been dead?" Gerstner asked.

"The cow two days and the sheep one," Penn replied.

"What was the state of the carcasses?" Dotty asked.

"The decay was moderately advanced," Penn said. "There was also scavenger damage."

"Could that account for blood loss?" Gerstner asked.

"Yes, it could," Penn replied.

"How much?" Dotty asked.

Penn shrugged. "I think the chupacabra took most of the blood. After all it was there first and made the kill. There was little blood on the ground, which leads me to believe the chupacabra drank the blood, leaving little for the scavengers to consume or spread around.

"One other item of note, other than the damage inflicted in taking down the animals, it seems the chupacabra inflicted no other injuries save for the neck wound. The other damage to the carcasses was consistent with scavenger damage. That seems to imply the creature prefers its prey to be living, rather than dead." He then folded his hands on his stomach. Mostyn took that as an indication he was finished speaking.

"Anything else for Dr. Penn?" Mostyn asked. There were no further questions.

Mostyn continued, "We're done for tonight. Make sure you read your reports. Tomorrow morning we'll be flying out of the Anacostia-Bolling airbase at ten o'clock. Don't be late. Good night."

The men filed out, Baker and Jones, however, stayed a moment to chat with Mostyn, Dotty, and Helene. Then they, too, left.

Helene hugged Dotty and kissed her cheeks. "My sister, how are you?"

"I'm not your sister," Dotty replied, "and I'm fine."

Puzzled, Helene said, "It is a term of endearment. You do not like?"

Dotty waved her hand. "Never mind." To Mostyn she said, "What was Bardon thinking?"

Mostyn shrugged. "The family that works together, stays together?"

Dotty shook her head, and turned to Helene. "You're okay with this?"

"The three of us working together?"

Dotty nodded.

"Oh, yes! It is a new experience!"

Mostyn chuckled and Dotty rolled her eyes.

Helene continued, "There are so many new experiences here in your world. It is so exciting. I could live forever, although I won't. I will die when my husband dies. But I love your world. For nine hundred years..." She sighed, then her face brightened. "I am working with Dr. Bardon to see if we can extend your lifespans. If we can, then I will get to live much longer with my husband and my sister."

"Stop calling him that. And I'm not your sister."

Helene had a big smile on her face, but there was an edge to the tone of her voice. "Dr. Bardon will use his ancient Egyptian magic again, if he has to. So play nice, little sister."

Dotty glowered at her.

Mostyn bowed his head and massaged his temples. After a moment, he lifted his head and spoke. "Look, ladies, let's get along. Shall we? Otherwise, this is going to be one very unpleasant mission."

"Sure, Mostyn. I promise I'll play nice."

"Good, Dot. Now let's get some rest. We have a long day tomorrow."

Walking out to his car, Mostyn couldn't help but wonder how Bardon thought this threesome would work. Initially Dotty had been okay with it, but of late... Well, time would tell if ancient Egyptian magic could tame Dotty Kemper.

4

WITH JONES AT THE WHEEL, the big black SUV burned up the miles following US 60 to the east and north from Phoenix. Their destination was a ranch outside the town of Foster, Arizona.

Bill and Judy Young owned an old spread of two hundred and eighty acres in Arizona just across from the Gila National Forest. They had a large herd of dairy goats and a small herd of milking shorthorns. They had also had a visit from the chupacabra.

In the front passenger seat sat Mostyn. In the second row of seats were Helene, Penn, and Gerstner. In the third row, Dotty, Ramsey, and Baker. As usual Baker was busy taking photos, in this case of the countryside.

Helene regaled the men sitting next to her with stories of life in the subterranean world of K'n-yan. Mostyn was looking over the computer files of all the reported sightings and attacks of both the chupacabra and the Jersey Devil. Dotty had a pair of earbuds in her ears and was reading. Ramsey was staring at and occasionally poking at his iPhone. Jones hummed some '80s song, every now and then augmenting Helene's stories.

The one thing about his team that Mostyn was very pleased about was that there was no young woman for Jones to hit on. Mostyn recognized that Jones was a good agent. The main problem with him, in Mostyn's mind, was that Jones looked like a Greek God and knew it.

The Fort Apache Reservation, through which they were driving, had a desolate feel about it. The land was hilly and brown and dotted with small trees and bushes. The grass looked dry and spiky. To the west of the highway there was periodically in view a cut in the terrain, evidence of a creek or maybe just a dry riverbed.

Mostyn couldn't help but think that a disservice had been done to the Native Americans. What the hell could they do with land this barren and dry? Unfortunately, war means there are winners and losers. True, the winners of the conflict often end up losing too. Their loss is just not as readily apparent. And in the conflict over who was to control the Americas, the native peoples had lost hands down. From Cortez to Captain Frederick H. L. Ryder and the Battle of Bear Valley in 1918, the Native Americans had consistently lost every war they fought with the Europeans and their descendants.

And now here we are, Mostyn thought, *dealing with beings from other dimensions. How are we not like the native peoples my ancestors conquered? Maybe the old saying is true: what goes around, comes around.*

Mostyn went back to reading the accounts of the chupacabra and the Jersey Devil and wondered if perhaps they were scouts for some inter-dimensional beings who would put earthlings on reservations.

———

Shortly before four in the afternoon, the SUV pulled up in front of the long, low ranch-style home of Bill and Judy Young. Mostyn had phoned ahead, so waiting for them was a man Mostyn guessed to be in his forties. He was wearing jeans and a flannel shirt, for the strong wind made the dry September air feel cooler than it was, especially when the sun slipped behind a cloud.

Mostyn exited the vehicle and walked up to the man. "I'm Pierce Mostyn, Special Agent in Charge." He showed the man his ID, which identified him as being with the Interior Department.

"I'm Bill Young," the man responded, shaking hands with Mostyn. Noticing the others in the SUV, Young said, "Why don't you and your team come inside?"

Mostyn indicated his team members should get out of the vehicle, and then they all followed Young into the house.

When seated in the living room, and after introductions had been made and coffee had been served by Judy Young, Bill got down to business.

"You want to know about the chupacabra. Well, it's real. After the first attack, Amos Brown, one of my hands, and I waited for it the next night. The moon was out so we didn't have any trouble seeing."

"When was this?" Dotty asked.

"Four weeks ago from last Thursday."

Dotty nodded.

Young continued, "Amos and I were in the back of the pickup, that way we could get a good shot. Along about one in the morning, we saw movement. Something was coming down from one of the hills. I picked it up in my scope. Looked like a she-bear in size."

"What does that mean?" Helene asked.

"It was around two-fifty to three hundred pounds." Young answered.

"Thank you," Helene said, and followed up with, "How do you know it was not a she-bear?"

"I was coming to that, young lady. I know it wasn't a bear because it had spines on its back and didn't have fur like a bear."

"Did you get a picture?" Baker asked.

"I didn't take a camera," Young replied. "I wasn't interested in getting its picture. I wanted it dead so it wouldn't be attacking any more of my animals."

Baker nodded. "I understand. Did you shoot it?"

"I shot it, but must've only wounded it. The thing took off before I could get in a second shot."

"What were you using, Mr. Young?" Mostyn asked.

"Bolt-action thirty-aught six."

Mostyn nodded. "And Mr. Brown didn't get in a shot?"

"He has that thirty-thirty lever-action and the creature was out about eight hundred yards."

"I see," Mostyn said. "How certain are you that you wounded the creature?"

Young looked perturbed. "Amos and I went back when it was daylight and found blood. That's how I know, Mr. Mostyn."

"No offense intended, Mr. Young," Mostyn replied. "You searched for the creature?"

"We did. Didn't find it, though. Blood trail just disappeared, and it got into some terrain where we couldn't follow its footprints."

Mostyn nodded. "And you haven't seen it since?"

"No, sir."

"In the remaining daylight," Mostyn said, "we're going to

do some searching on our own, if you don't mind showing us where you were when you shot the creature."

"Suit yourselves. But I doubt you'll find it." Young stood. "I'll get my truck. Just follow me."

————

A half-hour later found Mostyn and his team in a flat area of grazed prairie grasses and low, scrub-like trees, surrounded by several hills covered with similar vegetation.

"Up there, coming down from the top of that hill is where it was when I shot it," Young said.

"Jones, Ramsey, get the drones and set them loose," Mostyn ordered.

Ramsey looked up from his iPad. "*I'll* get them."

Jones shrugged. "Sure, Agent Geek. Whatever you want."

Ramsey gave him the finger, tucked the tablet into his backpack, and went to the back of the SUV.

Jones pressed a button on the key fob to unlock the back hatch and Ramsey took out what looked like a large suitcase. He extended the legs from one side so the case looked like a small table, then he opened it, got his iPad out, tapped on it, and out of the case flew over a hundred tiny drones.

Ramsey set up a second tablet that was stored in the suitcase and directed the drones in an ever widening circular search pattern for the chupacabra.

Young inquired of Mostyn what was going on.

"We're searching for the creature by means of those tiny drones. They have visual, infrared, and heat-seeking capabilities. If the creature is out there, Agent Ramsey will find it."

"But it could be anywhere," Young protested. "I shot it four weeks ago."

"I know. But it's possible the thing has gone to ground

somewhere to heal itself. If it has, Ramsey and his drones should find it. Otherwise I'll put money on it that he'll at least find the thing's carcass."

Young shook his head. "Well, I'll be damned. It's no wonder people are so paranoid over these drones."

"And they should be," Mostyn replied.

While Mostyn and Young chatted, the other team members got comfortable waiting for the drones to come up with something. All except Ramsey, Baker, and Helene, that is. Ramsey was busy with the drones. Baker was taking pictures with his camera, and Helene was reveling in the new experiences the locale was providing her.

Meanwhile the tiny drones continued to fly in ever widening circles. Ramsey bent over the tablets watching the data stream in. Mostyn, excusing himself from Young's company, joined Ramsey; although he couldn't tell much as to what was going on from the small tablet screens.

Mostyn checked his watch. The drones had been in the air for seventeen minutes.

"How much longer can they stay aloft, Ramsey?"

"Another two minutes and then I'll have to bring them back, sir."

"Okay," Mostyn replied.

And then a light began flashing in one of the small windows.

Ramsey got excited. "We have a heat signature, sir."

"The creature?"

"Possibly. The data stream indicates that whatever it is, it isn't your everyday ordinary coyote or gila monster."

"Do you have a location?"

"Yes. Putting it on this iPad now."

"Good, Ramsey. You may have just earned your paycheck for the week."

"The drone that spotted the heat signature has landed and is sending out a tracking signal. I've called the others back."

Mostyn called out, "Okay, people, listen up. We may have found the creature. Penn, get the tranquilizer rifle. Gerstner, get the cage. We'll be moving out as soon as the drones are back."

Within a few minutes the little machines returned and Ramsey safely stowed them away. Mostyn then gave the command to move out. He, Ramsey, and Penn were in the lead, Ramsey having a tracking device. The rest of the team followed, and even Bill Young joined them. He wanted to get an up-close look at what had attacked his animals.

The tiny drone's signal led them to a small rock outcropping. The creature was not immediately visible.

Young removed his baseball cap, scratched the top of his head, and said, "You think that thing buried itself and went into some kind of hibernation?"

"That's exactly what I think," Dr. Penn said.

"The signal is coming from under that ledge," Ramsey said.

Mostyn pointed to Gerstner. "Set the cage up. Dotty, can you help him? Baker, get your camera ready. Okay, Jones, let's dig this thing out."

The two agents started scooping away the dry soil. Penn was there, watching, with the tranquilizer rifle, and Baker was recording the operation. Helene was also close by.

"I think I have a thigh, here," Jones said.

The ground started shifting and Mostyn yelled, "Back!"

In a moment, the chupacabra had emerged from its hiding place. It wasn't fully awake and staggered on its feet. It let out a snarl and lunged for Jones, who was closest to the thing.

Penn fired his rifle and the tranquilizer dart bounced off the creature's furry hide.

Jones pulled his pistol out of its holster. The chupacabra

shook itself, let out another snarl, and made for Jones. Before he could fire his weapon, the thing disappeared.

"What the hell?" Young said.

And then the creature was in the cage Gerstner and Dotty had assembled.

"Who are you people?" Young asked.

Mostyn ignored the question and made a call.

"Mind my asking what kind of phone that is?" Young asked.

Mostyn turned to him. "Special satellite phone. We use it when there are no phone towers nearby. And to answer your other question, we are Interior Department people."

"Mighty handy contraption," Young said.

"It is," Mostyn replied.

Young stood there, baseball cap in hand, and said, "What I really want to know is how did you get that thing in the cage?"

Jones clapped him on the shoulder. "Pretty neat, huh?"

"Yeah, but how…?"

Jones smiled. "If I told you that, my friend, I'd have to kill you."

Young's eyes were like saucers.

Gerstner, Penn, and Ramsey had never seen Helene Dubreuil's ability to dematerialize things in action before, although they knew she could do so. Nevertheless, even with their knowledge, they were a bit wide-eyed as well.

"Chopper will be here in twenty," Mostyn said. "I suggest you all get comfortable."

With the chopper carrying the chupacabra and Dr. Penn on its way to a secret Federal facility, Mostyn decided to spend the night in Springerville due to the time being so late. They'd head out for Albuquerque in the morning, where they'd get the OUP jet to take them to their next destination.

Just outside of Springerville, there was a chain inn that had rooms and Mostyn had booked one for each of the team members. When they reached the big box building and entered the lobby, Dotty said, "You call *this* a hotel, Mostyn?"

Before Mostyn could reply, Gerstner said, "Well, it seems to me, Doctor, this inn is better than a roadside motel. At least it has wi-fi, TV, and serves breakfast."

Mostyn went to the desk to pay for the rooms and get the keys.

"I can't wait for tomorrow morning," Kemper replied. "Rubber eggs and gooey oatmeal. Yum."

Mostyn came back with the keys. "We're basically in the middle of nowhere, Dot. Be thankful they had rooms for us." He held out a key for her.

Helene was all smiles. "Besides, my sister—"

Dotty cut her off. "I'm not your sister, and I don't give a damn about the new experience. Got it?" She snatched the key out of Mostyn's hand and stormed off towards the elevator.

Mostyn shook his head and passed out keys to the other team members. They made their way to the elevator, Kemper long gone, and on the second floor began looking for their rooms.

"Here's mine," Gerstner said. He was across from Mostyn.

Jones and Ramsey had rooms down the hall. Helene was next to Mostyn.

"Are we going out for supper?" Gerstner asked.

"Half hour or so," Mostyn replied, and entered his room. He threw himself on his bed, and thought about the day's operation. It had been a success. They'd captured a living chupacabra. Bardon ought to be very pleased about that.

Bill Young had signed an agreement that he would not talk

about what he'd witnessed of the OLP operation. The penalty if he did so was that he'd be charged with treason against the United States of America.

"You people don't fool around," was his comment just before he signed. To which Mostyn had responded, "No, we don't."

There was a knock on the door. Mostyn got up to see who it was. Jones. He opened the door.

"Hey, Boss. Mind if Ramsey and I go get us all some food? We're starved."

"No, not at all. You have your agency card?"

"You bet. Want anything in particular?"

"No. Burger and fries. Otherwise, I'm okay with anything."

"Will do. We're off."

Mostyn closed the door and was almost back to the bed, when there was another knock. He walked back, saw Helene, and opened the door.

"Since it is still my month to be with you, let's look at the stars."

Mostyn smiled. "Sure."

He grabbed his suit coat and went outside with Helene. They walked a little way from the building.

"I do not think I will ever get tired of seeing the stars," she said. "And out here in the desert there are so many more to see. Every night is a new experience!"

Mostyn took her hand and chuckled. No stars, no moon, no sun in the subterranean world of K'n-yan. Just the never ending bluish light. And as far as Mostyn was concerned, they were welcome to it.

He thought back to the capture of the creature. The legend was not myth. It was real. Or was it? Penn and others would examine the thing of legend and decide just exactly what the creature was. Then they'd know for sure.

His thoughts, however, went to the night raid he and Kymbra NicAskill had conducted back in July. And Mostyn couldn't help but wonder if Van Dyne Corporation was somehow behind the chupacabra. The goat-sucker. That their enemy was right here among them.

5

THE CREATURE CHARGED him out of the pitch black night. It looked like a chupacabra, but was as massive as a four-story suburban mega-home. Mostyn fired his pistol, over and over, to no effect. This was it. The thing was almost on him, saliva dripping from its fangs.

All around him there was a ringing, and something was shaking him. The creature. He heard his name.

He opened his eyes. Helene was looking at him. "The phone is for you. Mr. Young says it is urgent."

Mostyn groaned, and took the phone from her. He noticed the time was 2:07 in the morning.

"Mostyn, here. What can I do for you, Mr. Young?"

"I think you and your people had best come back here right away."

"Why?"

"Because one of my hands, Pedro Garcia, was killed just a few hours ago. His throat was torn out. Which means there must be another one of those devil creatures out there."

Mostyn wondered if they were starting to travel in packs. To Young, he said, "Have you touched or moved anything?"

"Nope. Called you as soon as I could after we found the body."

"We'll be there as soon as we can. We're in Springerville. Did you call the sheriff?"

"Nope. Called you first."

"Good. Best if we leave the local folks out of this. My team and I will be there as soon as we can."

The call ended. Mostyn looked at Helene. She was sitting in bed in the buff as she usually was when she slept. God, she was beautiful. Long black hair. Flawless, alabaster skin. Small, perky breasts.

"You were having another nightmare. You should talk to Dr. Bardon."

"I have. Not much he can do. I've seen too many things. Done too many things."

She looked thoughtful.

"What is it?"

"I was just thinking. It is too bad I do not have access to K'n-yanian medicine. I am sure there is something that could be given to you so you do not have these dreams."

"Well, you don't," he replied. "So I guess I'll have to live with it. We'd best get going. Gotta get the others up."

"I'll call them while you get ready."

He looked at her. "How about we shower, and then call them?"

"Oh, Mostyn Pierce. You are a devil!"

"Maybe. Certainly not like the devil we're facing."

"What do you mean?"

"This is something new, and not new in a good way. The chupacabra isn't just going after animals anymore. Now it's attacking people. This isn't good. It isn't good at all."

————

Bill Young, Mostyn, and his team, save for Jones, who was at the Young home conducting interviews, watched as Dr. Dotty Kemper examined the body of Pedro Garcia. After a couple minutes, Mostyn turned to Young.

"So the first you knew anything was wrong, was when your ranch hand, Jimmy Two Feathers, came out to relieve Pedro."

"That's correct. Jimmy phoned it in. Had to drive about three-quarters of a mile to get a signal."

Mostyn nodded, and looked back at Kemper. "What do you think, Dot?"

She was stooping next to the body, a small and powerful flashlight in her hand. "He didn't put up much of a fight. I'd say he was caught by surprise. Arms show signs he tried to defend himself. The attacker bit into and then tore out that section of his throat. Kind of like a dog or wolf might do. The jugular vein and carotid arteries were severed. He would have died very quickly. There's very little blood on the ground, so I'm guessing that when we get him in for the autopsy we'll find he was exsanguinated by the attacker."

"I better arrange for a chopper," Mostyn replied. He motioned for Young to follow, and while they walked a short distance from the group Mostyn made his call to OUP head-quarters. When finished he turned to Young.

"Keep this quiet."

"Sure. I understand."

"Did Pedro have family?"

"He wasn't married. But he did have a girlfriend. He lived at home with his parents and four siblings."

Mostyn keyed in the data on his phone. "Address?"

Young gave him the address, and Mostyn keyed that into his phone as well. Then he sent a text with the data to head-quarters.

"I'm not sure what the official story will be, but you will be briefed. The young man's body will have to be examined, so my superiors will come up with a cover story. I assume I needn't remind you about the papers you signed."

"No, sir, you don't."

"Good."

"So that thing, the chupacabra, it's going after people now," Young said.

"Won't know for sure until we do an autopsy."

"So what am I going to do, Mr. Mostyn?"

"A team will come in to look for this new creature. We're very interested in finding it. Once found and removed, hopefully things will go back to normal for you."

"I hope so. Enough is enough. Coyotes and big cats are bad enough. We don't need any bloodsucking devil creatures."

"On that, I think we agree."

———

Three hours later Dotty Kemper and Pedro Garcia's body were on their way to a secret Federal facility. An hour after that an OUP team arrived on the Young property to hunt for the chupacabra. Agent Ramsey was assigned to assist the new team, and Willie Lee Baker stayed to take pictures.

Mostyn, Jones, Helene, and Gerstner bid their teammates goodbye and got in the big black SUV. Jones got the vehicle on the main highway and pointed it in the direction of Albuquerque and the OUP jet waiting to take Mostyn and company to their next destination.

"Looks as though the chupacabra might have to be renamed," the mythologist said. "They aren't simply the goatsucker any longer."

"That's going to be a major bummer," Jones said, "if this thing develops a taste for human blood."

"That it is, Jones, that it is," Mostyn replied.

Helene took his hand. "You are worried Mostyn Pierce."

"Yes, I am."

"You do not need to worry. You will find a way out of this."

He squeezed her hand. "I don't know, Helene. At least the beings that threaten us from outside this universe are easily identifiable. It's the monsters within ourselves, they are the ones, I think, that will ultimately destroy us."

6

ONCE AGAIN MOSTYN found himself in New Jersey's Pinelands. Jones guided the big black SUV west from Atlantic City International Airport. Penn and Kemper had rejoined the team at the airport. Dusk was gradually darkening the September sky.

Gerstner was discussing Penn's preliminary findings. "So if I understand you correctly," the mythologist said, "the chupacabra is a man-made creature."

"That's correct," Penn replied. "We analyzed the genome. It's had DNA spliced in from at least eight different animals, including humans."

"What did it start out as?" Dotty asked.

"That's where the touch of irony enters the picture," Penn said. "It started out life as a bear."

Dotty laughed. "A bear? Oh, that's choice."

"Isn't it, though?" Penn replied.

Mostyn turned to Dotty Kemper. "Would you give us an update on the results of your autopsy?"

"I emailed everyone an abstract," she replied. "What the situation looks like to me is that the victim was taken by surprised, made a meagre attempt to defend himself, and had a chunk of his throat ripped out.

"The force used was considerable. This is a very strong creature.

"Since there was not a lot of blood showing on the ground, I'm assuming the creature drank the victim's blood. Approximately ninety-five percent of it, allowing for initial loss and what I found remaining in the body."

"Anything to identify the attacker?" Mostyn asked.

Penn answered. "Dotty sent me the analysis of the saliva found around the wound. It's a match for a chupacabra."

Mostyn closed his eyes and leaned his head back against the headrest. After a moment he opened them, and asked, "Can the work be traced back to Van Dyne Corp?"

"Possibly," Penn answered. "If we can find DNA in the creature that no one else is using, then that would be an indicator Van Dyne's hand is in this."

Mostyn nodded. "There's been a new development."

"When did you find this out, Mostyn?" Dotty asked.

"Just before we landed at Atlantic City. Bardon texted me. There have been three attacks in three days on farms near Jeremiah's Peak, a little hamlet north and east of Hesstown, here in New Jersey. The third attack occurred last night. The victims were a dog, a sheep, and a pig, in that order. The attacks are very similar to the chupacabra's, but according to the two eyewitnesses the creatures were tall, hopped like a kangaroo, and had bat-like wings."

"The Jersey Devil," Gerstner said.

"So it seems," Mostyn agreed.

"And the attack signature was the same?" Baker asked.

"Apparently."

Penn ran his hand through his hair. "That would indicate minds that are the same, even though the bodies are different."

"Match the form of the creature to the local legend," Mostyn said.

Gerstner nodded. "Makes a lot of sense. The chupacabra in areas with a high Hispanic population, since that is where it first appeared, and the Jersey Devil in its old stomping ground of New Jersey Pinelands legend."

"What is the purpose of this?" Helene asked.

"That is the sixty-four thousand dollar question," Mostyn replied.

"Why is the question worth sixty-four thousand dollars?" The puzzlement in Helene's voice and on her face was genuine.

"It was an old TV game show," Dotty said.

"Oh, I will see if it is on YouTube," Helene said, a big smile on her face.

"Don't bother," Dotty replied. "The show was rigged."

"Rigged? What is 'rigged'?"

"It means the producers of the show didn't play fair," Dotty said.

"Oh." The look on Helene's face clearly indicated she didn't have the slightest notion as to what Dotty was talking about.

"The question before us," Mostyn said, "TV game shows aside, is to what end is Van Dyne producing these creatures? What purpose do they serve?"

"What does Van Dyne do with the other things it creates?" Jones asked.

"Don't know for sure," Mostyn answered. "I suppose legitimate sales. Van Dyne Corp produces all manner of genetically modified items. So I suppose those are all for public show and tell. As for these monsters..." Mostyn shrugged. "What I do know is that no corporation engages in R and D if they aren't going to end up using, or at least hope to use, the results.

Research and development is expensive. Corporations want to get their money back. After all, the whole reason they're in business is to make money."

"Piles of it," Jones added.

"Right," Mostyn replied, "which gives credence to the rumors that van Dyne wants to sell these monsters to militias, revolutionary groups, organized crime, any bad guy who can pay his price in order to create mass chaos so the thugs can take over. Bardon, however, is holding his cards close to his vest on this one. Consequently, it's all just a guess."

"Okay, it's a guess. What are we going to do about it?" Dotty asked.

"Talk to people and see what we can find out," Mostyn said. "And run a little surveillance on Van Dyne, since we'll be in the neighborhood."

"I don't mean to change the subject," Ramsey said, "but where the heck are we?"

"New Jersey," Jones said.

"I know that, wise ass," Ramsey shot back. "Where in New Jersey? There's not a single streetlight and we haven't seen another vehicle for at least fifteen minutes."

"Welcome to the Pinelands," Gerstner said. "The place where legends are born."

"This isn't *The Twilight Zone*, dude," Ramsey said. "One moment we're in civilization and the next we're in the middle of nowhere."

"Everyone thinks New Jersey is an extension of New York City," Mostyn explained. "That's true to a great degree for Northern New Jersey. Southern New Jersey is different. While I wouldn't call it wilderness, there are an awful lot of trees and there are definitely fewer parking lots."

Jones slammed on the brakes. The vehicle swerved, but he kept it from going into a skid.

"What the hell, Jones?" Dotty yelled.

Outside of the vehicle the night was dark. The headlights shone down an empty road. Jones sucked in a great quantity of air, ran his hand over his face, and let the air back out.

"What is it, Jones?" Mostyn asked.

"I..." He took in a deep breath and exhaled. "We almost hit it."

"Hit what?" Mostyn said.

"The Jersey Devil."

7

Mostyn and the others got out of the SUV. Flashlights stabbed the darkness.

Ramsey swung his flashlight in a wide arc. "God, I hate trees."

"I'm with you there," Dotty said. "Can't see a goddamn thing."

"Jones, get the lights out of the back," Mostyn ordered.

"Sure thing, Boss."

Jones went to the back of the SUV, opened the hatch, and got out two boxes. Each one was about the size of two shoeboxes. He set one box on one side of the SUV and aimed it towards the woods. He flipped a switch, and said, "Let there be light!"

The beam of light the small lamp put out was equal to one of those great big old searchlights. Jones set up the other lamp on the opposite side of the SUV and in a moment that section of highway looked like the sun had forgotten to set.

Jones called out, "There you go, Agent Geek and Dr. Asphalt. Light. Plenty of light."

"All right, people," Mostyn began, "spread out. Let's see if we can find some footprints or other evidence, so we know that Jones wasn't just hallucinating."

"Gee, thanks, Boss."

"Don't mention it," Mostyn said, while clapping Jones on the shoulder.

After twenty minutes, their search had picked up nothing save for a couple of footprints.

Dotty seemed disappointed. "I guess we can't blame our sudden stop on you being crazy, Jones."

"Love you, too, Kemper," he shot back.

Baker photographed the prints, and Mostyn ordered the team back into the SUV. Jones stowed the lights.

When they were once again driving down the highway, Gerstner asked, "I wonder if it was on its way to or from its target?"

"We'll probably have an idea if we hear of another attack tomorrow," Mostyn said.

"In a way, it's too bad you didn't hit it, Jones," Penn said. "Would have given us something to compare to the chupacabra we captured."

"Yeah, well, I'd just as soon not have to fill out the accident report," Jones replied.

"Yes, you upper-worlders love paperwork," Helene commented. "Until I met Mostyn Pierce, I had not touched paper and pen for two hundred years."

Jones looked at the rearview mirror. "Amazing what a difference just a couple miles can make."

"Oh, yes, DC," Helene replied. "The new experiences are endless."

"So how did the government work in your world?" Ramsey asked.

"In K'n-yan there is no government. At least not like you upper-worlders seem to think you need. Our customs and traditions dictate what is and is not acceptable. We do not need someone to tell us that." She paused, and then said, "*They* do not need someone to tell them what to do. *I* am one of you now."

In a few more minutes they rolled into the New Jersey city of Vineland and the GPS directed Jones to the Vinegate Hotel, the only three-star hotel in a sea of expensive two-stars. Herndon, the accounting wonk, had made sure to point out to Mostyn that he was putting them in the best hotel available.

Jones pulled into a parking spot and everyone got out.

"What is this place?" Dotty said, her voice dripping disdain.

"Look, Kemper," Mostyn said, "Herndon said this was the best place to be had and made sure to tell me to tell all of you he did his best."

"He's an accountant," Dotty shot back. "What the hell does he know besides numbers?"

Mostyn sighed. "No complaining. At least they serve a hot breakfast."

"Big whoop-de-do. I don't eat breakfast," Dotty said.

Jones had a big grin on his face. "Maybe you should, Kemper. Might improve your disposition."

"Fuck you, Jones."

"No, thank you."

Sniggers and choked laughter rippled through the group. Dotty grabbed her bag and stormed off towards the hotel entrance, flipping the bird to everyone in her wake.

Mostyn walked over to a van that was parked in a corner of the parking lot, obscured by shadows. As he approached, a door opened, and out stepped Dr. Bardon. A wave of sweet Virginia pipe tobacco came with him.

"Good evening, sir."

"Good evening, Pierce, my boy."

The two men shook hands. Bardon had a yacht-shaped briar pipe in his mouth, which he slipped into his pocket.

"You don't need to do that on account of me, sir."

"That's all right, my boy. Smoked out. Ready for a little surveillance work?"

"Yes, sir."

"Good." Bardon rubbed his hands together. "Who's coming with us?"

Mostyn looked at the little round man in his Brooks Brothers suit, complete with homburg, and said, "You're going out into the field?"

"Why not? A leader should not be afraid to do what he asks his people to do."

"The situation could, um…"

"Go pear-shaped?"

Mostyn nodded.

"Boy Scout motto, Pierce. Be prepared. I have a Level Four EDT handy just for such situations."

Mostyn raised his eyebrows in surprise. The Emergency Defense Talisman 4 was quite powerful. To summon one also involved a healthy withdrawal from the blood bank.

"Oh, I know what you're thinking, my boy. Don't you worry. There will probably be no need to use it. Now, who's going with us?"

"I think Jones."

Bardon thought a moment, and said, "Too heavy."

"Heavy? You're not—"

Bardon was all smiles. "SNOB Two is on its way." He looked at his watch. "Should be here in ten minutes."

"If you want someone lighter, that leaves Dotty or Helene."

"Yes, it does. So which one?"

"Dotty's more experienced."

"True. However, Helene has that wonderful ability to dematerialize."

"She does. But I think I'd rather have experience."

"Okay, my boy, Dr. Kemper it is. Get her and let's be on our way."

———

SNOB-2, being larger than SNOB-1, had greater payload capacity. Mostyn looked at all the equipment on board, and even given the greater lift ability, was surprised the blimp could get off the ground.

Piloting the craft was Special Agent Delphe Bird. A little wisp of a woman. Mostyn thought she could have had a great career as a jockey, if she'd been so inclined.

Dotty and Bardon were seated in the back and discussing possible modifications to the human genome.

Up ahead was the Van Dyne building. Mostyn corrected himself. One of the Van Dyne buildings. This was their public face. They had secret facilities scattered around the world, and not even Bardon knew where they all were.

Special Agent Bird piloted the blimp to a position eight hundred feet above the building. "We're here, sir," she informed Bardon.

The OUP director rubbed his hands together, his face radiating excitement.

"Good, good. The first thing we'll do is release the cyborgized mice drones. Come, Pierce, help me."

Bardon opened a case in which there were five rows of small mouse-like entities, five cyborgs to a row. The director pressed a button on his laptop and twenty-five little mammalian machines woke up. Mostyn and Bardon tossed the little things out one of the blimp's windows, and watched them fly down to the Van Dyne building.

Dotty Kemper, who'd been watching, asked, "What on earth are those things?"

"Our little spies," Bardon said. "Those highly modified mice will do what mice normally do, and oh, so much more."

"Are they carrying transmitters?" Mostyn asked.

"Yes," Bardon replied. "Whatever those little mouse ears pick up, their hearing having been cybernetically enhanced, will get transmitted back to us."

"What happens when we aren't here?" Dotty asked.

"That comes next," Bardon said, and held up a small sphere. He pressed a button and out of the sphere came two rotors and four small legs.

For all the world, Mostyn thought the thing looked like a little helicopter.

Bardon set the sphere on the floor, tapped a few keys on his laptop, and the rotors began spinning. The thing lifted off and flew out the window of the blimp towards the Van Dyne building.

"What's it going to do?" Dotty asked.

Bardon answered, his stance a bit like that of a professor in front of his class. "It will attach itself to the side of the building, the rotors will drop off, and then it will open into a dish antenna. That's how we will be able to listen in when we are not here physically."

"That's pretty amazing."

"Glad you think so, Dr. Kemper. I'm rather proud of these little gadgets. Been very useful."

"You've used these before?"

"Oh, yes, my boy. Trial by fire, so to speak. Trial by fire."

"How come I never knew about them?" Mostyn sounded a bit put out.

"Need to know basis. Need to know."

Bird's voice broke in. "We're going to get company, sir."

"Get us out of here, Ms. Bird. Pronto."

"Yes, sir."

Mostyn and Dotty looked out a window as ballast fell from the blimp and the twin props began spinning at high rpm. Taking off from the roof of the Van Dyne building were three creatures with large bat-like wings. Bardon joined Mostyn and Dotty at the window.

"They're sending the Jersey Devil creatures after us," Bardon said.

The blimp banked sharply to starboard. The creatures flew surprisingly fast, and we're rapidly closing the distance.

"We need more speed, Bird," Mostyn called out.

"I have this thing going flat out. Sixty miles per hour is it."

"Get the wind behind us," Mostyn replied.

"What wind, sir? There isn't any."

"What's our armament, Dr. Bardon?"

"One fixed light machine gun facing forward. This wasn't intended for combat. Don't worry, my boy. I have the EDT Four." Bardon took out his phone and began tapping on it.

The blimp bounced.

"I think the devil has landed," Dotty said, and took her pistol out of its holster.

Mostyn picked up his suppressed submachine gun and returned to his window.

"We're losing gas pressure, sir," Bird called out.

"Keep us aloft as long as you can, Ms. Bird," Bardon replied.

One of the creatures flew towards Mostyn's window.

"I can't believe how big these things are," he said, and then pulled the trigger. In two and a half seconds, Mostyn had emptied the magazine and the bullet riddled body of the creature was plummeting towards the ground.

Special Agent Bird brought the nose of the blimp up in an attempt to use aerodynamic lift to compensate for the gas the airship was losing.

Another creature grabbed onto the side of the gondola, and reached for Dotty with one of its claws. She fired four rounds into its long neck and the creature fell to Earth.

"Where's the third devil?" Mostyn asked.

"I see it in the rearview camera, sir," Bird called out. "Looks like it's just following us."

"Probably relaying our position to van Dyne so we have a welcoming committee when we crash," Dotty said.

"You are undoubtedly correct, Dr. Kemper," Bardon said. "However, I'm almost done here." He made a couple more taps and a shimmering green aura surrounded the sinking airship.

"Looks like we're in the middle of an aurora borealis," Dotty said.

"What took so long?" Mostyn asked.

"This particular inter-dimensional being decided it wanted to renegotiate, rather than follow protocol. Given our current situation, it was simpler to negotiate. However, that Class Two Xenophage hasn't had the last laugh. No sirree Bob!"

"Dr. Bardon, I can't keep her in the air much longer. The rent in the fabric must be getting larger."

"Hm. I suppose so," Bardon said. "Airflow and all that. How much time, Ms. Bird?"

"About a minute."

"Very well. Put out a mayday and let's prepare for impact."

Dotty and Bardon sat in the aft seats and put on their seat belts. Mostyn got into the seat next to Bird, and belted himself in.

With the nose of the blimp angled up, Mostyn looked out the side window. The New Jersey landscape was coming up fast and everywhere he looked he saw trees. This was not going to be a pretty landing.

Special Agent Bird throttled back the electric motors and the airship's forward movement slowed. She flipped a switch and dumped the rest of the water ballast. When the water was gone, she turned off the electric motors.

The airship shuddered as though a myriad of hands were grasping it. All Mostyn saw were trees. Then all was still and portions of the envelope slowly draped themselves over the gondola.

Looking out the window, Mostyn saw deciduous trees and evergreens and part of the envelope of the blimp. The trees, as it were, had taken hold of the gondola and the envelope and were gently holding them. He turned to Bird, "I have to say, that was the softest crash landing I've ever experienced."

She did a little bow from her seat. "Thank you, Special Agent Mostyn. Now, since I'm the lightest, I'm going to see just how far off the ground we are. Sit tight."

Bird unbuckled her seatbelt and moved aft. "Dr. Bardon, Dr. Kemper, are you two all right?"

"Fine," Kemper said.

"Nice flying," Bardon replied.

"Thank you, sir."

Bird opened the emergency hatch in the floor and looked down at the ground. The shimmering green aura made it look as though the ground was moving.

"What's the verdict, Bird?" Mostyn asked.

"Can't tell for sure, sir, due to the aura. I'll guess about twenty-five feet."

"We can use the cloud car to get down to the ground," Bardon said.

"We probably don't want to do that, sir," Mostyn said. "We're safer inside the EDT."

"I can re-deploy it once we're on the ground."

"And if it gives you fits like before?"

"I see your point, my boy. Very well, we'll stay here for the time being."

"However, I'd like to go to the ground and get a better idea of our situation," Mostyn said. "I can do that, right, Dr. Bardon?"

Bardon nodded. "Yes. We can leave the defense bubble. It just prevents other things from entering."

In the distance, they heard howling.

"Hear that, Mostyn?" Dotty said. "I think you have your answer."

Mostyn turned to Special Agent Bird. "How far are we from the Van Dyne building?"

"About a half-dozen miles or so, sir."

Mostyn pursed his lips, and stared out the window. After a moment he spoke. "I guess we sit tight and wait. Let's hope our guys get here first."

They sat and waited, while listening to the howling grow ever closer. After five minutes passed, Mostyn got out of his seat and moved aft. The gondola shifted, but didn't fall any further.

"Looks like we're stuck pretty good," Bird said.

"Looks like it," Mostyn concurred.

He loaded the submachine gun, and grabbed three additional magazines. Turning to Bird, he said, "How do I get to the cloud car?"

"Is this necessary, Mostyn?" Dotty asked. "The cavalry should be here any time now."

"They should, but they might not. Bird, the entrance?"

"That hatch at the very back of the gondola."

Mostyn went to it and opened it. He peered into the opening and saw a seat surrounded by a space no bigger than that of the soap box derby racers he played with as a boy. He shook his head and got in. He just fit.

"Okay, Bird, lower me. I want to be about ten feet off the ground."

"Mostyn, we have the EDT. This is no time to play cowboy." Dotty's voice contained a slight note of worry.

Bardon spoke up. "They shouldn't be able to get through the talisman, Mr. Mostyn. I quite agree with Dr. Kemper."

The howls were getting louder.

"That may be, sir, but I'd still like to know what we are up against. And the only way to know that is for someone to get clear of the blimp, so we have a three hundred and sixty degree surveillance circle. Night vision binoculars, please."

Bardon handed the binoculars to Mostyn. "When you leave the blimp and pass through the aura, the Xenophage will mark you and that way you'll be allowed to come back through. The marking might sting."

"Thanks for letting me know." Mostyn signaled for Bird to lower the car. A hand telephone set connected the car with the gondola.

Passing through the aura he felt sharp needles stabbing him all over his body. He looked at his hands and saw they left no mark. When he thought he was ten feet off the ground he told Bird to stop.

From the car, he took a good look at the terrain surrounding the airship. Trees. Nothing but trees as far as he could see. The howling was very close now. Dozens of voices sounded. Whatever was making the noise had traveled very fast. He scanned the area circling the airship. Nothing but the trees. He started a second sweep and that's when he saw them making their way through the forest. It was as if Van Dyne Corporation had unlocked the gate to hell.

8

Mostyn moved the selector on his weapon to two-round bursts and opened fire on the three-headed dog charging towards him out of the trees. At the same time, Special Agent Bird pressed the button and the winch began pulling the cloud car back up to the gondola.

The dog collapsed in a heap. Three Jersey Devils leaped for the car. Mostyn fired. One fell to the ground, writhing. The other two held onto the car, their talons piercing the thin metal. The winch whined in protest over the extra weight.

Mostyn fired point blank into the face of one of the creatures. The 5.7mm rounds shattered the thing's head and it fell away. The other creature clawed Mostyn and knocked the submachine gun from his hand.

With his left hand, Mostyn retrieved his back-up pistol from the small of his back and emptied the magazine into the thing. It uttered a scream and Mostyn watched it fall to earth.

A two-headed ogre-like monster charged out of the trees firing a machine pistol with one hand, and swinging a massive club with the other. Mostyn returned fire with the submachine gun just before the cloud car rejoined the gondola of SNOB-2.

Bullets from the machine pistol, intended to rake the underside of the gondola, vaporized in the shimmering green aura.

From one of the windows, Dotty opened fire with her pistol. The ogre staggered and then collapsed in a heap.

More Jersey Devils flew out of the night and were vaporized by the EDT when they attempted to grab hold of the blimp.

Mostyn climbed out of the cloud car and joined the others at the windows.

Bird pointed. "Look! Something's up."

In the clearing, an array of Cerberus dogs, giant wolf-like things on two legs, two-headed ogres, Jersey Devils, and a centipede the size of a refrigerator with a human face had suddenly stopped, as if instantly frozen.

With their heads cocked at an angle, it was apparent they were listening for something. After a moment, they turned and melted away into the surrounding forest. In the distance Mostyn and the others could make out the sound of helicopters.

"It's about time the cavalry got here," Dotty said.

"Good thing, too," Bardon said, looking at his phone. "This cantankerous Xenophage is ready to call it a day."

———

The District of Columbia is filled with nondescript office buildings which house the two to three hundred thousand bureaucrats who help run the Federal Government.

In one such nondescript building, the Office of Unidentified Phenomena is housed. And in one of its conference rooms a meeting was being conducted.

Dr. Rafe Bardon was seated at one end of the table and

Special Agent in Charge Pierce Mostyn at the other. Mostyn's team members and three OUP works filled in the rest of the chairs situated on the sides of the table. Insulated pots of coffee and boxes of doughnuts decorated the middle of the table. Bardon had his own insulated pot filled with tea.

The conference room was decorated in Modern Federal Sterile. Everything white, save for the beige carpet. No one, though, seemed to care about the room's decor. Not when there was coffee, and more importantly doughnuts. Especially doughnuts paid for by the boss and made by Mike's Doughnut Shop.

When the coffee and doughnut ritual had been performed and a break in the chitchat occurred, Dr. Bardon began the meeting.

"Two things are now very apparent," he said. "The first is that the chupacabra and the Jersey Devil are man-made creatures."

The wonks scribbled away on their notepads. They were using notepads because Bardon preferred paper over computers. His thinking was that it's pretty difficult to hack a sheet of paper.

Coffee cup halfway to his mouth, Dr. Penn, the forensic veterinarian, added, "GMO animals, as it were. Genetically modified organisms." The coffee cup continued its journey.

"Yes, indeed," Bardon said.

There was more scribbling.

"What I can't figure out," Gerstner, the mythologist, began, "is why anyone would want to create these things in the first place. They don't serve any useful purpose, except perhaps to arouse a primal sense of fear."

Around a bite of doughnut, Dotty said, "That may be their purpose. To instill fear."

"Very true, Dr. Kemper," Bardon said. "Which brings us to

the second thing we know. The Van Dyne Corporation is the one creating them."

Pens and pencils duly noted that point.

"Along with a whole host of other lovelies," Mostyn said.

Bardon chuckled. "Indeed."

"Maybe they are entertainment," Helene said, "since you don't have slaves."

One of the wonks looked up, thought he was going to say something, and then changed his mind.

"I don't think so," Mostyn replied. "Van Dyne Corp is planning something. The question is, what?" Mostyn noticed that Bardon was deliberately playing ignorant. Giving little tidbits and nothing more. The question that immediately came to his mind was, why?

"The cyborg rodents we sent them should give us valuable information," Bardon said.

"In the meantime, what do we do, sir?" Mostyn asked.

Bardon drank tea and puffed on his pipe before answering. "A slight change of plans is in order, which is why I've called you here. I think we should let our little cyborgs do their job, and in the meantime you take your team to North Carolina and find out what Van Dyne Corporation is doing there."

"That seems like a waste of time, Dr. Bardon," Kemper said. "We know Van Dyne's creating these things, let's deal with them on their home turf."

Bardon knocked the dottle out of his old bent bulldog, and put it in a pocket. From another pocket he extracted an apple-shaped pipe and began filling it from his tobacco pouch. "True, Dr. Kemper. We are now fairly certain the Van Dyne Corporation is behind the creation of the chupacabra and the Jersey Devil. Well, at least the current incarnation of the Jersey Devil. However, we don't know why and we don't know where they create them."

Pipe filled, Bardon lit it, and began puffing away. Although technically no smoking was allowed in the building, Bardon didn't seem to be bothered by the technicality. And no one dared say anything.

The OUP director continued, "The New Jersey facility is their public face. They do very little of their real work there. Although, as Mr. Mostyn can attest, and you yourself, Dr. Kemper, the fruits of their labors can be seen there. If you are at the facility at the right time."

"But if we—"

Bardon raised his hand and stopped Dotty Kemper from continuing. "North Carolina. You leave tonight. Anything else?"

Kemper shook her head. Bardon looked at the others. More head shaking and a "no" or two were voiced.

"Well, then, we're done here." Bardon stood and exited the room. The wonks closed their notepads, pocketed pens and pencils, and followed the director out.

Baker stood, stretched, and snagged another doughnut. "Know where we're going in North Carolina, Boss?"

"I do. A little town called Pine Bluff. Nestled in the beautiful hills of Appalachia."

"You're kidding," Jones said, "we're going back *there*?"

"Not kidding, and, yes, we are," Mostyn replied.

Helene stood. "It is not West Virginia, DC. No abhumans."

"They're all abhumans down there," Kemper said.

Gerstner, a smile on his face, replied, "You're going to get in trouble one of these days, Dr. Kemper, for not being even a little PC."

Kemper stood, took a doughnut, and poured herself a cup of coffee. Then said, "Is this the face of someone who cares?"

Gerstner chuckled. "I guess not."

"Good. We're on the same page." She turned to Mostyn

and Helene. "Come on, you two, we have to pack some traips-
ing-in-the-goddamn-woods clothes. Shit."

9

WHILE MOSTYN and his team were on their way to North Carolina, Dr. Bardon was sitting in his office. He lit his pipe, and when he had it going, he flipped a switch and a large screen descended from the ceiling along the wall opposite his heavy black walnut desk. He tapped a few keys on his computer and the screen came alive with thirty windows.

Twenty-five of the windows provided information from the cyborgized mice. The other five windows provided various views of the Van Dyne headquarters building. And at that moment, over two dozen OUP analysts and agents were also observing what Bardon was looking at.

One mouse was assigned to each of the fifteen floors and one to each of the three basement levels. The remaining seven mice roamed at will or were directed to specific locations to provide extra sets of eyes and ears.

Bardon gazed at each window, noting where the mice were and what they were observing. Since the time was late, well after normal business hours, as well as after the cleaning crews had left, there was nothing to hinder the mice from having free rein of the building.

After seeing what each mouse was observing, the OUP director focused on mice numbers eight and nine. They were the ones assigned to the floors Mostyn and NicAskill had damaged. He could see that the floors were well on their way towards being operational again.

"What are you up to, Valdis Damien van Dyne?" Bardon whispered to the display. "It can't be anything good."

The director switched his attention to the mice assigned to the basement levels, and noticed the mouse on Sublevel 2 had entered a room by traveling through the ductwork and in between the walls. Bardon brought up a schematic of the floor.

"Aha! As I thought," Bardon murmured. "This room is unknown. Perhaps a later add on."

Bardon watched what the mouse was seeing with interest. The room was obviously some type of laboratory. The question, of course, was what manner of experiments were conducted there.

Perhaps I was wrong, Bardon thought, *and Van Dyne does do some of their major research here. Hopefully, the mouse will give us a clue.*

He messaged the supervisor of the mouse controllers and asked that three more mice be directed to the room. The secret lab was dimly lit and there wasn't much detail Bardon could make out.

"We will definitely need to have eyes and ears on this place when there is work going on," he murmured.

He brought up all of the mouse windows again to see if there were any more surprises the little cyborgs were finding. While he watched, he noticed the windows for mice nine and eleven go dark. Then, in rapid succession, the mice — all of the mice — were running helter-skelter, as though they were trying to get away from something.

Bardon messaged Dan Marche, the controller's supervisor. The text read, "What's going on?"

Three more windows went dead while Bardon typed. The phone on his desk rang.

"Bardon."

"Dr. Bardon, Dan Marche here. I have no idea what's going on. The mice are in predator response mode."

"Predator? What predator?"

"Don't know, sir."

"Well, find out. Pronto."

"Yes, sir."

Bardon cradled the receiver and watched as the windows went dark one by one. He noticed the screen for mouse number four. In front of it was a snake. A very large snake. Bardon didn't recognize the species and suspected it had been genetically modified. The snake lunged and the window for mouse four went dark.

He leaned back in his chair. Somehow Van Dyne had learned of the mice and prepared a countermeasure. A very effective countermeasure.

Images blurred across the last remaining window. The mouse was literally running for its life.

"Go little mouse. Go!" Bardon whispered.

Then it stopped, and the screen went dark. Bardon sighed, got up, and walked to the sideboard situated between the statues of Cthulhu and Shub-Niggurath. He poured himself a glass of port, and returned to his chair.

He took a sip of wine and was about to shut down the video feed, when the screens all came alive. The scene was as though one was looking at fog. Then slowly, out of the fog, a face became visible. It was the face of Valdis Damien van Dyne. His mouth began moving and Bardon enabled the audio.

"...you appreciated my little display tonight. It would behoove you, Dr. Bardon, to stop interfering with the operations of my company. People more powerful than you can imagine are interested in my results. So go play somewhere else and leave me alone. If you don't, you may wake up one morning and discover your little department no longer has any funds to operate. And you don't want that, now, do you?"

The face faded away into the fog and then the windows went black.

Dr. Bardon leaned back in his chair and sipped his wine. He knew van Dyne was well-connected. If his tentacles reached as far as he intimated, there could be problems. Big problems. Bardon finished his port and stood. Time to pay a visit to his secret library, hidden away in sub-basement four. It was time to fight fire with fire.

10

THE DRIVE to Pine Bluff was long. Thank goodness the scenery made up for the length of the trip.

Mostyn thought the view was much like what they'd seen driving to Heirloom, West Virginia about a year ago. Beautiful, with an underlying feeling of unease.

Baker sat up front next to Jones and was photographing the scenery. Being September, the trees were only beginning to show a bit of color. Baker had to content himself with photographing a lot of green. Jones, as usual, was humming the tune to some '80s song.

In the second row of seats were Mostyn, Dotty, and Helene. Mostyn was reading reports on his tablet. Dotty was sleeping, her head on Mostyn's shoulder, and Helene was looking out the window, pointing at, and oohing and aahing over, everything.

Drs. Penn and Gerstner, in the third row of seats, were discussing mythical creatures and the possibility of them having once existed. Agent Ramsey was seated next to Gerstner. Oblivious to the scenery and discussion, he was playing a video game on his phone.

Having flown into Pope Army Airfield late the previous night, Mostyn thought it best if everyone got some sleep. The team stayed overnight in a hotel in Fayetteville, and left for Pine Bluff early in the morning. Mostyn let a smile play on his lips. Herndon, the accounting wonk, would have a cow over the extra expense.

Between the town of Murphy and the unincorporated village of Marble, tucked into the hills, was the hamlet of Pine Bluff. Right in the middle of North Carolinian Appalachia. And the site of recent chupacabra sightings.

Helene interrupted his thoughts. "Oh, Mostyn Pierce, look at all the colors! And everything is so bright! K'n-yan is very, very dull compared to our world."

He smiled at her. "It is. Nothing save that wretched blue light down there."

"And here, we have the blue sky. It is so brilliant." She sighed. "I could live forever…"

He touched her cheek. "Don't think about it. Just live each day. Experience it to the max. A famous philosopher once said, 'Life is like a story: what matters isn't how long it is, but how good it is.' Make life good, and it will be long enough."

She put her hands on his cheeks. "You are so wise, Mostyn Pierce, is it any wonder I love you?"

Baker, in a loud whisper, said, "Hey Jones, pull over at the next motel. Those two need to get a room."

Jones laughed. "Sure thing. The Boss has—"

Mostyn interrupted. "Very funny, you two. Very funny."

Helene pointed. "Look! There's a motel in five miles."

Laughter shook the SUV, woke up Dotty, and made Ramsey look up from his game.

"What's going on?" Dotty asked.

"Nothing, Dot," Mostyn answered.

Jones, however, wasn't going to let Mostyn's comment stand. "The horn toads want to stop at the motel coming up."

Dotty gave Mostyn a look, said, "Shit", and rested her head on the window.

Jones and Baker burst out laughing. Penn and Gerstner smiled. Ramsey went back to his game.

A puzzled Helene asked, "What's a horn toad?"

Laughter once again shook the SUV.

Shortly before noon, the SUV pulled into Pine Bluff. Mostyn put away his tablet and looked at the cluster of buildings making up the tiny unincorporated hamlet.

"Where do you want to park, Boss?"

"Good question, Jones," Mostyn replied.

Ramsey, looking up from his phone, said, "This is a town?"

"Park by the store," Mostyn said.

Jones complied, and, when he shut off the engine, everyone got out.

"Is this it?" Dotty asked.

"Probably," Baker said. "You have your convenience store, and a couple of gas pumps. A laundromat, three bars, two churches, and a bunch of houses."

Ramsey let out a laugh. "Houses? These are trailers."

"Mobile or prefab homes," Baker corrected. "And don't be so snooty. Do you live in a mansion?"

Ramsey gave Baker the finger and went back to his phone.

Baker, on the other hand, started taking pictures of the place.

Amazement and wonder was all over Helene's face. "This is so—"

Dottie interrupted, "Yeah, we know. Exciting." She turned to Mostyn. "Start by asking in the store?"

"Sure, Dot. You and Helene. Jones, I want you and Ramsey to take the bars. Penn, Gerstner, you guys see if there's anyone at the Methodist church. Baker and I will check out the Baptist church. Meet back here when you're done."

Mostyn and Baker started for the church.

"So, Mostyn," Baker began, "any idea why Bardon shuffled us off to this little bit of nowhere?"

"Nope. No idea whatsoever."

"After all, wouldn't there be more to find back in New Jersey?"

"One would think so, Willie Lee. One would think so."

"It's like that old hymn we sang when I was a kid. Bardon moves in mysterious ways, his wonders to perform."

Mostyn let out a laugh. "Isn't it supposed to be 'God'?"

A smile tugged at the corners of Baker's mouth. "Huh. I guess it is."

Mostyn noticed the sign in front of the church. Christopher Hayes, Pastor, was in fairly big letters. Underneath the pastor's name were the times for Sunday School and worship. Below that was "Going About As A Lion." Mostyn guessed that was the sermon title.

The two men climbed the four steps to the porch and tried the double doors. The latch moved and the door on the left opened when Mostyn gave it a push. He and Baker entered, the latter calling out, "Hello! Anybody here?"

There was no narthex. The doors opened directly into the semicircular auditorium. The pulpit was on a bit of a thrust stage, allowing the preacher to be partially surrounded by his audience.

"I like this layout," Baker said. "Kind of puts the pastor in the middle of his flock. Instead of the usual, he's up there, we're back here, and he preaches *at* us."

"Huh. Hadn't thought of that. Got a point, there, Willie Lee."

Again they called out, "Hello", and asked if anyone was around.

A door opened to the side of the pulpit area, where the organ was located. A man of average height and looks, much like Mostyn, emerged.

"Hello. How can I help you?"

"Are you the pastor?" Mostyn asked. "Reverend Hayes?"

"I'm Christopher Hayes. How may I help you gentlemen?"

Mostyn and Baker walked up to him and shook hands. Mostyn continued, "We're looking for information about the recent attacks. The chupacabra?"

Hayes looked puzzled. "What did you call it?"

Baker repeated, "Chupacabra."

Mostyn took a picture out of his coat pocket and handed it over to the minister.

Hayes looked at it. "The locals have run across a few of these creatures. Thought they were some kind of unknown bear species. In fact, Jethro Kemp shot one a week ago. Roasted it on a spit. Invited the whole town to his place for a potluck picnic. I was a bit leery at first, but the eating wasn't bad. Kind of tasted like chicken. Jethro said it was quite mean and the hide was very tough. Managed to shoot it in the eye. That's the shot that finally stopped it."

Mostyn and Baker looked at each other, then back at Hayes. Mostyn spoke. "We've had reports of several attacks by these creatures."

"I think someone somewhere got something confused. Why don't you come to my office, and we can talk there."

Mostyn and Baker followed Reverend Hayes to a room

behind the auditorium. The pastor indicated chairs where they could sit. Hayes sat on the sofa situated between the chairs.

"Your names are?"

"Sorry. I'm Pierce Mostyn and this is Willie Lee Baker. We're with the Interior Department." Mostyn reached inside his coat for his ID, but Hayes held up his hand and shook his head.

"The creature I think you are probably more interested in, Mr. Mostyn, is what we call the Lessing Vampire."

"Lessing Vampire?" Baker said.

"Yes. The Lessing Vampire has plagued this area for generations. This chupawhatever is a new comer. The locals aren't too concerned about it."

Mostyn's eyebrows reached for his hairline. "Really?"

Hayes nodded.

Mostyn shook his head and shrugged. "Okay. So where does this Lessing Vampire come from?" Mostyn asked.

"Goes back to before the Revolutionary War," Hayes said. "Several families moved out to this area to settle it. Wilderness back then. Not even many Native Americans were around here. The families were Catholic and wanted to escape the persecution they were suffering at the hands of their Protestant neighbors."

"Some things never change," Baker said.

"No, they don't," Hayes replied. "Humanity's intolerance for anything different seems to be one of our defining traits."

"So it seems," Mostyn said.

Hayes nodded, and continued with his story. "As things so often happen, a young man, Richard Argeneau, fell in love with an older, married woman. Mary Channing. They were caught 'in the very act of adultery', as one record puts it, and were tried, found guilty, and sentenced to death by the priest, Father Lessing."

"Lovely," Mostyn said.

"Intolerance was more brutal then, Mr. Mostyn," Hayes said. "It still exists, of course. It's just that we're more subtle now. More genteel."

Mostyn and Baker nodded.

The minister continued. "Mary Channing was branded with the letter 'A', strangled, and then burned at the stake for being a witch. She was strangled as an act of mercy because her husband was a man of some importance."

"And the young man?" Baker asked.

"Instead of repenting and asking forgiveness for his sin, as Mary had, he cursed the church and renounced his faith. Father Lessing cursed Argeneau in return, asking God to give him a restless soul. Then, in an attempt to get Argeneau to recant his rejection of the church, he was tortured by pressing. The reports say Argeneau cursed God with his last breath."

"He must've really loved her," Baker said.

Hayes shrugged. "I suppose."

"And that's it?" Mostyn asked.

"Oh no," Hayes replied. "Ten days later, Mary Channing's husband died. Supposedly there was a bite mark on his neck and his body was drained of blood. Argeneau's grave was dug up and it was empty."

"Interesting," Mostyn said.

Hayes nodded. "The legend of Father Lessing's Vampire persists to this day. The recent attacks have given it new life."

"So you've had recent attacks by the chupacabra *and* this Lessing Vampire?" Mostyn asked.

"We had a couple by the...," Hayes paused, then went on, "chupacabra. Some reporter must've picked up on them. However, we haven't had any since Jethro shot that one. But the recent attacks by the Lessing Vampire have been vicious."

"Has anyone seen this vampire?" Mostyn asked. "Because we haven't heard of it at all."

"A few claim to have seen it," Hayes replied.

"What does it look like?" Baker asked.

"Depends on who you talk to. It looks something like Bela Lugosi's portrayal of Dracula all the way to a sort of wolf-like creature that mostly walks on two legs."

"A bit of a difference there," Mostyn said.

Hayes smiled. "That there is. The old women seem to see Bela Lugosi."

Mostyn chuckled. "Interesting. You said the attacks were vicious. How so?"

A mild shudder took hold of the minister. "Bodies ripped apart. Some partially eaten. However, most just had the blood sucked out of them."

Mostyn made a mental note to pass this information on to Bardon as soon as possible.

"How come we haven't heard about these attacks?" Baker asked.

Hayes smiled. "The locals are very superstitious. They also don't care much for outsiders." Hayes let out a chuckle. "One might say, what happens in Pine Bluff stays in Pine Bluff."

Baker laughed and a smile touched Mostyn's lips.

"Anything else, gentlemen?"

"Are there any research facilities around here, or factories?" Mostyn asked.

Hayes shook his head. "No one's much interested in development here. And the tourism people and conservationists aren't interested in any development getting a start either. Nor the locals."

Mostyn continued. "Any businesses owned by outside interests?"

"Not that I'm aware of," Hayes said. "There is, though, the Vautier place."

"Tell me about it," Mostyn said.

"Old Rowland Vautier died some twenty years ago. He was a hundred and one and had no heirs. The house, mansion actually, stood empty for five years. And then someone bought it. A fellow named Jarvis Worthly. No one's ever seen him. Although there have been comings and goings from the place in the fifteen years he's owned it. But no one can get close to the property. There are armed guards, patrols, an invisible fence, and a physical one."

"Doesn't that strike you as odd?" Baker asked.

"Oh, very much so. The Vautier place is the subject of much gossip. But no one can find out anything as to what's going on there. Although three years ago, five boys from the junior high found a way into the place. A cave that apparently connects to the cellars."

"What did they discover?" Mostyn asked.

"Nothing. Some monsters scared them and they left. So they said, anyway."

"Interesting," Mostyn replied, putting on his best poker face. "Do you know who the kids were?"

"Billy Vicks, I think, was one. You could ask the store owner, Lester Rabren. He knows most everything that goes on around here."

Mostyn stood. Baker and Hayes followed. "You've been very helpful, Reverend," Mostyn said, extending his hand to the pastor.

Hayes shook hands with him. "Glad to. Hope you find what you're looking for."

Mostyn and Baker left the way they'd entered. On the way out, Baker said, "You think Jarvis Worthly is a front for Van Dyne?"

"Do bats fly at night?"

11

THE BIG BLACK SUV bounced down the rutted and potholed gravel road. Jones skillfully negotiating to minimize the impacts of the jolts. Mostyn and Baker were in the back seat, doing their best to hang on.

"What the hell do they spend their taxes on?" Baker asked.

"Not on roads out in the country," Jones said.

From Lester Rabren, Mostyn had gotten the names of the boys who'd been out to the Vautier place, as well as directions to the old mansion. He also managed to talk to two of the boys, but neither one was willing to go anywhere near the place. No matter the inducement Mostyn offered them.

"I don't *never* want to see one o' them monsters ever again," one of the boys declared.

He was, however, more than glad to tell Mostyn how to get to the cave in exchange for the twenty bucks Mostyn offered him.

Armed with both pieces of information, Mostyn decided he, Baker, and Jones would check out the Vautier estate while the rest of the team canvased the houses in the village for information. He also tasked Dotty with booking reservations for the night at the casino-hotel just outside of Murphy.

Jones guided the SUV around a pothole and slowly rolled into and out of a pair of ruts. Fifteen feet further on a clearing occurred in the wall of trees and undergrowth. The sign announced the drive was private and that visitors were not welcome. Jones stopped.

"Now what, Boss?" he asked.

Mostyn and Baker got out. Willie Lee snapped pictures while Mostyn searched the sides of the drive. Eight feet in he found what he was looking for: the two receptors and the faint red line of the laser beam, positioned about two inches above the drive.

He walked back to the vehicle. Jones had gotten out and was chatting with Baker.

Mostyn informed them about what he'd found.

Baker took a picture of a squirrel. "We're on the west side of the property and there's another drive on the southeast side. Right?"

"Correct, Willie Lee," Mostyn said. "And the cave entrance is up on the northwest corner of the estate, not far from the creek. If the boys are telling us the truth."

"Only way to find out is to take a look."

"Right, Jones," Mostyn said, "so let's get going."

They got back into the SUV and bounced their way over a couple more miles of road.

"Stop," Mostyn said. "This must be the boulder the kids spoke of. Supposedly the opening is just straight back from here, in the side of the hill."

Jones stopped the vehicle and shut off the engine. Everyone got out.

"Baker, I want you to stay with the car," Mostyn said. "Jones, let's take a look. Keep your eye peeled for laser alarm triggers and any other warning devices they may have set up."

"Gotcha, Boss."

The two agents plunged into the forest and within a dozen steps had lost sight of their vehicle.

"I don't think I've ever seen trees this thick. Not even where we were last year," Jones said.

"One of the densest forests I've ever seen," Mostyn replied.

They proceeded cautiously looking for any alarm triggers.

Jones tapped Mostyn and pointed. Mostyn followed Jones's finger and saw a small camera mounted on a tree.

"Good eye, Jones. Good eye."

"So now what, Boss?"

"We now know they have surveillance cameras, in addition to laser-triggered alarms. I think we go back, wait until dark, and make another attempt."

"They might have stuff to see intruders in the dark."

"They might, Jones, they might. In fact, they probably do. But I think we just chance it and see what happens."

"Fine by me. Do we have any of Bardon's special toys?"

"A few."

Jones rubbed his hands together. "Cakewalk."

———

Shortly after midnight the SUV stopped by the boulder. Mostyn, Jones, Ramsey, Dotty Kemper, and Helene Dubreuil got out of the vehicle. They were dressed in black and had headsets to connect them to Ramsey. The white sliver of the moon was high in the sky.

Ramsey set three small drones on top of the SUV and in a moment they were flying into the woods. Mostyn and Jones looked over Ramsey's shoulder and watched the screen.

As though talking to himself, Ramsey murmured, "Phase one, take out the cameras."

Mostyn watched a tiny lightning bolt leap from the drone to the camera. This was repeated three more times.

"Okay," Ramsey said, "Cameras are down. Now for the lasers."

The drones flew another twenty or so feet into the woods and zapped the lasers.

"This section of their electronic surveillance field is down," Ramsey said.

"Good," Mostyn acknowledged. To the others, he said, "Let's go. Ramsey will keep us informed if the drones spot any problems. We're going to take a look-see, and then leave."

The four walked into the forest. The two women in the middle of the line, with Jones on one end, next to Helene, and Mostyn on the other next to Dotty.

The forest canopy was dense and blocked out the meager light from the moon and stars. The drones, flying some fifty feet ahead of the OUP operatives, were winking in the manner of fireflies. There was no underbrush to speak of, due to lack of sunlight. But there were plenty of sticks, fallen tree branches, rocks, and holes to catch the feet. Not even the night goggles were of much help.

Helene sent her thoughts to Mostyn. *Mostyn Pierce, my husband, perhaps I should dematerialize and go on ahead.*

Mostyn sent his thoughts back to her. *Not yet. We don't know what Van Dyne might have waiting for us.*

Very well, my love, Helene replied.

The group made slow progress and in twenty minutes had only walked about three hundred feet into the forest, every-one, save Helene, tripping or falling at least once.

Jones, slowly placing his foot into a depression, whispered to Helene, "How come *you* haven't tripped or fallen?"

She sent her thoughts to him. *Due to the dimness of K'n-yan's light compared to the upper world's, I have better night vision than you.*

Jones grunted back an acknowledgment and focused on carefully placing his feet.

Ramsey's voice sounded in their ears. "The drones are picking up heat signatures. They're coming in fast from two o'clock."

Mostyn pulled out his phone, tapped an app, typed four characters, and a pale green bubble surrounded them. Moments later six three-headed dogs charged out of the trees. Giant beasts that Mostyn guessed must weigh five or six hundred pounds.

The creatures skidded to a stop at the sight of the bubble, and Kemper raised her machine pistol.

"No," Mostyn commanded. "The bullets won't go through the aura."

"What is it?" she asked.

"Tactical Defense Field. Level Eight."

"Eight?" Jones said.

"Yep," Mostyn replied. "Bardon insisted."

One of the Cerberus creatures leaped for the agents and vaporized when it hit the aura.

"What do we do now?" Dotty asked.

"We wait and see what they do. A Level Eight field is not mobile."

"Not mobile?" Dotty shouted. "What the hell, Mostyn?"

"Bardon's idea, Dot, not mine."

"Him and his goddamn toys," Dotty muttered. "He needs to give us what we need to do our job."

"We're safe, Dot. What more do you want?"

"I want to be able to get the hell out of here, Mostyn. Is that too much to ask?"

"Let's see what happens," Mostyn replied.

"I'm so done with this goddamn organization," Dotty muttered.

Jones chuckled. "What are you going to do, Kemper? We can't quit."

"No, we can't," she replied. "But I sure as hell don't have to go out on any more of these goddamn assignments. 'Field work,' he said. Field work, my ass."

"Look, Mostyn Pierce."

Everyone followed Helene's pointing finger. Standing between two trees was a nightmarish giant.

"What the hell is that thing?" Jones said.

"It must be ten feet tall," Dotty added.

The creature had the body of a man, with an extra set of arms. The head was on a longneck, and just above the nose slits was one very large compound eye. The thing lifted an arm, the palm of its hand facing the green bubble. In the palm, was an eye. A cat's eye.

"What's it carrying?" Dotty asked.

"I think we're about to find out," Mostyn said. "Everyone down."

The thing lifted a large tube affair, aimed it at the Tactical Defense Field, and pulled the trigger. A glowing white ball shot out of the tube and hit the green field. The field flickered, and, for just a moment, at the spot where the white ball struck, the field disappeared.

"What is that thing?" Jones said.

Dotty checked her machine pistol. "A non-mobile defense field. Of all the stupid…"

In their ears, Ramsey's voice sounded, "I'm coming to the rescue."

Two drones flew up to the giant's head, and little lightning bolts shot out of the drones. The little arcs of electricity touched the monster's skull. The thing roared, clapped two hands to it's head, and fell to the grcund.

More drones appeared. The dogs began snapping at the little machines. A set of jaws caught one of the drones and chomped it. A cluster of the little machines surrounded the beast and zapped it with lightning bolts. The huge creature dropped to the ground. The remaining three-headed dogs ran off, the drones in pursuit.

"Okay, people, time to fall back." Mostyn said. He tapped some keys on the phone and the green field disappeared. "Let's go. Use flashlights."

Four flashlights flicked on, and in their beams stood four very tall wolfish-looking creatures. And they were standing on their hind legs.

12

DOTTY KEMPER FIRED FIRST. The soft choo-choo-choo sound of her suppressed machine pistol sounded loud in the night. Two of the monsters expired in that initial shower of lead. Blood, flesh, and bone spraying the forest floor.

The remaining two creatures charged the OUP operatives. One creature took down Jones, the other leapt at Helene and met nothing but air. The creature on Jones vanished and rematerialized inside a tree, its face just visible. Dotty shot and killed the remaining monster.

"Holy shit," Jones said, as he got up from the ground. "That thing was strong."

Helene rematerialized.

"Thank you," Jones said, as he touched Helene's arm.

"You are welcome, DC," she replied.

Mostyn watched Jones's lingering hand and a dark cloud passed over his face. He shook his head. "Okay, people, let's get out of here before they throw more surprises at us."

"What I want to know is why Agent Geek didn't warn us," Jones said.

They heard in their ears, "Sorry about that. Didn't see them appear on the screen. And fuck you, Jones."

Jones just shook his head.

"We should take one of these creatures back with us for study," Dotty said. "It's probably the Lessing Vampire people are talking about."

Mostyn nodded. "Probably should."

"We can't carry it," Jones said. "Not if we're planning on booking it."

"I'll do it," Helene volunteered. She and one of the creatures dematerialized.

"I have *got* to learn how to do that," Dotty said.

"Then maybe—"

"Shut up, Mostyn. I know what you're going to say."

"Fine, Dot. Let's get out of here."

Mostyn, Kemper, and Jones turned on their flashlights and made good time getting back to the road. A couple of times Mostyn thought he'd heard something, almost like the slithering of a snake. But a sweep of the flashlight behind them revealed nothing.

When they reached the vehicle, Ramsey and Helene were packing away the last of the drones. The body of the Lessing Vampire was in the back of the SUV.

To Ramsey, Mostyn said, "Drop those." To everyone, he said, "Into the vehicle. Now."

Ramsey started to protest, and Mostyn yelled, "Now!"

Ramsey dumped the drone case and remaining drones in the back of the SUV, closed the hatch, and got in the back seat.

With the team in the vehicle, Jones made a difficult U-turn, and drove back to the village as fast as the rutted and potholed road allowed.

"What's on the agenda now, Mostyn?" Dotty asked. "They foiled our plans pretty good back there."

"We get the creature back to civilization for study. Then we discuss the information we've obtained thus far, and find out from Bardon what he wants us to do. Quite frankly, I think we pretty much have one option."

"Which is?" Dotty prompted.

"We have to destroy the labs where these things are being made."

"Do we know where they are?" Helene asked.

"Nope. Not all of them. But I bet this place is as good a bet as any to be one of them."

———

In spite of the early morning hour, the casino still had customers. Mostyn was able to secure the use of a small conference room, and ordered coffee and pastries to refuel his team.

On the way back to the casino and hotel, he had phoned in and requested a helicopter to pick up their package. By the time the SUV had reached Murphy, a chopper was en route to their location. Forty minutes later, Penn and the Lessing Vampire were on their way to a secret Federal facility.

For an hour, the team, minus Penn, discussed their findings, drank coffee, and ate pastries. When there was nothing left to discuss, Mostyn summarized where they were at.

"What it seems we have thus far," he began, "is a lot of gossip."

"And misinformation that even Bardon took for fact," Dotty added.

Mostyn nodded. "Yes, there is that. But we've located four people who have fairly credible sightings. Two of them lost animals to the creature: a dog and a goat. There's also a pig farm that suffered losses several miles from here. Lots of rumors, but no eyewitnesses. And then we have the guy who shot the chupacabra and ate it."

Baker interrupted. "Don't forget the kids."

Mostyn took a sip of coffee, and nodded. "I'm getting there. Thanks, Willie Lee. The killing of the animals, and vague accounts of the sightings, fits with the other information we've collected on the chupacabra and the Jersey Devil. There is nothing really new here, other than the physical form of the Lessing Vampire, which differs from both the chupacabra and the Jersey Devil. Albeit all three are vampiric entities, in that they bite their victims and suck their blood."

"As I said before," Gerstner began, "Van Dyne Corporation matches the creature's form to that of local legend. I think we can assume the chupacabra to be the base form. They then modified the creature for New Jersey and here."

"I think that's a reasonable description of what Van Dyne is doing," Mostyn said.

"But we still don't know why." Jones devoured a pastry.

"No, we don't," Mostyn said. "And we might never know. Unless we can get hold of the project files. Going with the rumor mill, the intended use is not good. Now, the most interesting part of all of this is what those kids saw. They were able to get through the woods and enter a cave, which connected with the mansion's cellar."

"Van Dyne's plugged that hole real good," Jones said, while picking up another pastry.

Mostyn nodded, sipped coffee, and continued. "That they have. What scared the kids were monsters. They described them as creatures out of some video game. They made loud noises and chased them back out through the cave and the woods."

"And you don't think they made it up?" Dotty asked.

Mostyn shook his head. "No, I don't think so. I don't see

any reason why they should make up something like that. And our own encounter with monsters tonight seems to confirm their story."

"So what do we do now?" Gerstner asked.

Mostyn took a sip of coffee. "I think the decision is up to Bardon. If we are to take direct action against the Vautier mansion, we need an assault team. And Bardon needs to okay sending one."

"That's what you're going to recommend, though, isn't it?" Jones said.

"Yes. We don't know what Van Dyne Corp is up to. But none of the creatures we've encountered are looking for a role in *Beauty and the Beast*. I think they should be stopped before they start implementing whatever it is they're planning."

"Fine with me," Jones said.

"Everybody okay with that recommendation?" Mostyn asked.

The team members nodded or gave a thumbs up.

"Okay," Mostyn said. "Get some sleep. I'll send in my report to Bardon."

The meeting broke up, but instead of going directly to his room, Mostyn walked outside.

Such a beautiful place, he thought. Why is it that beauty is often merely a façade and that what is real is unimaginable ugliness and horror?

13

CONGRESSWOMAN DIANE STEINBERG, phone to her ear, did not look at all happy. She was what in times past was called a handsome woman. Her large, hawk-like nose prevented her from being considered beautiful and at fifty years of age that bothered her. Though not as much now as when she was young. However, in lieu of youth and beauty, she did have power and money. Both of which could entice many a man to her bed. And at her age, she was too old to bother with getting a nose job. She'd gotten to where she was today without one, and she could stay on top of her mountain without one.

However, the man on the other end of the phone was not such a one that could be enticed into anyone's bed with mere power and money. He was a puppet master. He was the one who made the marionettes dance.

"I understand, Mr. van Dyne," the congresswoman began, "however, until five minutes ago when you mentioned the name, I was not even aware of the existence of the Office of Unidentified Phenomena." There was a pause, and then she continued, "I will look into the situation, Mr. van Dyne, and... Yes, yes, I'll make sure they redirect their efforts elsewhere."

Another pause, and then Steinberg took a deep breath before speaking. "Of course, I realize you are my top contributor, sir. I assure you I will do whatever is necessary. Yes. Thank you, Mr. van Dyne. Goodbye."

She cradled the receiver. "Goddamn pompous prick. Of all the gall...," she muttered.

Diane Louise Steinberg stood and looked out her office window at the buildings below. Eleven-term congresswoman from California. Chair of the House Judiciary Committee's subcommittee on Crime, Terrorism, Homeland Security, and Investigations. She was a person to be reckoned with.

The Congresswoman looked at her nails. *Time for a manicure*, she thought. *I'm overdue. Too damn busy.*

She returned to her desk, sat, opened a drawer, and took out the bottle of bourbon and a glass. She poured herself two fingers of whiskey and drank half of it in one gulp. She grimaced at the alcohol burn.

For all her power and control, for all the strings she pulled on her own marionettes, she herself was just another puppet. Her master was Valdis Damien van Dyne, and he wanted her to stop the Office of Unidentified Phenomena from harassing Van Dyne Corporation. But she'd never heard of the office, or its director, Dr. Rafe Bardon. Van Dyne knew more about the agency than she did. Maybe there was some truth to the existence of these deep black op organizations that not even the President could access.

She pressed the button on her desk to summon her chief of staff. In a moment, a woman opened the door and poked her head in. "You rang?" she said.

"Miriam, I need you to find out everything you can on a Dr. Rafe Bardon. He is supposed to be the director of the Office of Unidentified Phenomena. Have you ever heard of either?"

Miriam cocked her head in thought for a moment. "No, ma'am."

Steinberg nodded. "See what you can find out. And I need the information yesterday."

"Yes, ma'am. Anything else?"

"No. And, Miriam…"

"Yes, ma'am?"

"This has top priority over everything."

"Yes, ma'am. I'll get the information."

———

Across town, Dr. Rafe Bardon was looking at the tea and fry up his secretary Evelyn, had brought him.

"Heaven on earth," he muttered. He stabbed a fried mushroom with his fork, just as there was a knock at the door and Evelyn poked her head in.

"Sorry to disturb you, sir. But Mr. Parker is here to see you. He says it's urgent."

Bardon frowned. What did Parker want this early in the morning? And why couldn't he have called? The frown disappeared, and Bardon sighed. "Send him in." Bardon ate his mushroom.

Evelyn closed the door, and in a moment there was a knock.

"Come," Bardon said.

In strode a tall man, with thinning sandy-colored hair.

"Have a seat, Mr. Parker," Bardon said. "I'm at breakfast. I hope you don't mind."

Parker waved his hand. "No, go ahead. Please."

Bardon smiled his thanks, and speared a piece of sausage. "What is so urgent?" He popped the sausage into his mouth.

"We've gotten wind that Miriam Abramowitz is trying to find out about you and the OUP."

"Has she had any success?" Bardon guided a forkful of scrambled egg to his mouth.

"We don't think so, but she has an uncanny ability to sleep with the right people and get the information her boss wants."

Bardon swallowed a bite of fried tomato. "And who is that?"

"Her boss?"

Bardon nodded.

"Congresswoman Diane Steinberg."

"Ah, yes, now I remember." Bardon speared a sausage, took a bite, chewed, and swallowed. "Thank you for letting me know, Mr. Parker. This probably has something to do with Valdis van Dyne, doesn't it?"

"He has been phoning senators and congressmen, and probably everyone else he controls."

"As I thought. Grab a snake by the tail and the head will thrash about. I will take care of Miriam Abramowitz, Mr. Parker. Do keep me informed."

"I will, Dr. Bardon."

Bardon watched the Assistant to the Under Secretary of Homeland Security for Intelligence and Analysis leave, and took another bite of sausage. When he'd swallowed, he buzzed Evelyn on the intercom.

"Yes, sir?"

"Come, please."

"Be right there, sir."

In a minute, Evelyn entered Bardon's office.

"Evelyn, there is a woman, Miriam Abramowitz, who is Congresswoman Diane Steinberg's chief of staff, I believe. I need some of her hair. Please dispatch an agent to procure that for me as soon as possible."

"Yes, sir."

Bardon watched Evelyn leave, and then drank tea. He turned his gaze to the hideous statues of Cthulhu and Shub-Niggurath that were on either end of his sideboard. He addressed them as if they were his students.

"We know so much, and yet we know nothing at all. For our knowledge is fragmented by the artificial disciplines we've created. If all knowledge were brought together in but a single discipline, all of humanity would end up insane — or gladly retreat into a new and permanent dark age."

14

MOSTYN WAS ANGRY. He stared at the tablet. His team sat around the conference table waiting for what he had to say. He re-read the revised orders from Bardon. A Major Clement C. Beauregard would be arriving soon with a detachment of fifty OUP Special Forces operatives. Major Beauregard's mission was to seize the Vautier property and everything on the property. Mostyn and his team were relegated to clean-up. They'd make sure the Major and his men hadn't missed anything.

"I don't like this one bit," he muttered. To his team, he said, "We've been set on the bench. Bardon's sending in an OUP Special Forces team."

"Why?" Jones asked.

"No explanation," Mostyn replied.

"Come on, Mostyn, you know why," Dotty said. And when he didn't say anything, she continued, "He's afraid his 'best people' might get hurt."

"We've been in far more dangerous situations," Mostyn replied.

Jones yawned and stretched. "So what's stopping us? Can't we get in before the Special Forces goons?"

Mostyn gave Jones a long look, his face thoughtful. Finally he said, "How?"

"Well, for starters," Jones began, "we have your wife, Ms. Stealth. Special Forces don't have her abilities."

Helene clapped her hands and jumped up and down. "Oh, yes, Mostyn Pierce. I can dematerialize and clear the way. It will be so exciting."

"A new experience," Dotty said, her tone mocking. She also rolled her eyes.

Helene turned around and faced Dotty. "You are being mean."

"And why shouldn't I be? You stole my man. Even Jones is calling you his wife."

"Well, I—" Helene didn't finish the sentence. Dotty's right fist shot out and hit Helene in the chest. Her left upper cut connected with the underside of Helene's chin, snapping the K'n-yanian's head back. Helene sank to the floor glassy-eyed.

Mostyn ran between the two. "For God's sake, Dotty."

"She deserved it," she shot back.

Helene shook her head. Mostyn knelt down. "Are you—?"

She pushed him aside, and stood. She wobbled a bit, but caught her balance. "That was not nice, Dotty Kemper. *You* are not nice."

Dotty took a step towards Helene and vanished.

"Helene! No!" Mostyn yelled. "Please." He stood. "Please, Helene."

She looked at him, took a deep breath, and exhaled. "Very well, my husband."

Dotty reappeared and Helene slugged her. Dotty reeled back and fell on her butt.

"Holy shit," Jones said, "a cat fight."

"Shut up, Jones." Mostyn's tone was sharp.

"My money's on Helene," Ramsey said.

"No money's anywhere. You two will stop it right now. We're on a mission." Mostyn squatted next to Dotty.

"Are you all right?"

"Save it, Mostyn. You can fuck that bitch all you want. I'm done." Dotty got up, and stormed out of the conference room.

Mostyn looked up at the ceiling, and muttered, "Why now? Why the hell now?"

———

Mostyn went for a walk. He needed to get away. Have some time to himself. There were walking paths from the casino and hotel into the woods. He took one. Maybe Mother Nature would give him some wisdom.

He had no idea what to do about Dotty and Helene. He'd tried to talk to Dotty, but she wouldn't let him in her room and told him in no uncertain terms that he could go and copulate with himself. He didn't pursue trying to talk with her. She needed time to calm down first.

Helene, on the other hand, felt slighted; that he was favoring Dotty.

Mostyn shook his head, and muttered, "Women. You can't live with them and you can't live with them."

And then there was Jones. Jones the Greek god playboy and Jones the cowboy.

Mostyn didn't like the playboy. He didn't like the little gestures he made to Helene, and even at times to Dotty. Mostyn did, however, like Jones the cowboy. The Jones who would rather ask for forgiveness than permission. And he liked Jones's idea for this mission. All Bardon needed to do was give him a couple more agents and some high-powered weaponry and Mostyn could pull it off. Whatever happened to doing more with less?

He was inclined to play the cowboy. But now, with Dotty and Helene at each other's throats, he no longer had a functioning team. And that pissed him off even more than Bardon's new orders.

There was a bench. He sat down, put his head in his hands, and sighed. He'd leave, except no one really left the OUP. Too secret. If you could work, they gave you a desk job. If you couldn't work, they packed you off to a quiet, isolated place with a pension. And you were under constant surveillance.

He didn't relish a desk, and he didn't want big brother watching his every move. This thing, though, between Dotty and Helene was getting him down. He was beginning to think it was match point to Kemper. Bardon and his magic had failed.

What to do? What on earth was he going to do?

15

Special Agent in Charge Pierce Mostyn was once again sitting at the table in the small conference room in the casino and hotel on the outskirts of Murphy, North Carolina. He'd just finished briefing Major Clement C Beauregard, who was pacing up and down the length of the room.

Beauregard turned, stopped, and said, "Thanks, Mostyn. Now here is the plan. At Oh Five Hundred we'll hit the Vautier place with an EMP."

"Won't that destroy valuable records?"

Beauregard continued his pacing. "Might. However, we need to knock out their ability to respond."

"Van Dyne uses genetically modified organisms, monsters, if you will, to respond. They're not going to use missiles."

"I know that, Special Agent Mostyn. I've read your reports and the other data on Van Dyne Corporation. So I know they use electronic surveillance, and I want it knocked out before my men go in. Those people need to be blind so my people can do their job with the least amount of casualties."

Mostyn leaned back in his chair, laced his fingers behind his head, and closed his eyes.

His thoughts ran over the Major's statement. An EMP would do too much damage to sensitive data. Of course, critical areas might be in a Faraday cage. Might. If Van Dyne had anticipated a direct assault. At the headquarters in New Jersey, certainly. Out here in the sticks? Probably not. No one knew about this place. Secrecy was the protection here.

He opened his eyes and looked at Beauregard's back. "There's a better way."

"What's that, Mostyn?"

"Send my team in first to secure the sensitive data."

"Too risky. That's why I'm here."

"So you'd rather destroy the data." Mostyn stood, and faced the major, who was now walking towards him. Mostyn continued, "Data Dr. Bardon wants and *needs* if he's to stop Van Dyne."

"Need I remind you, my orders are from *Bardon* and they are to take the facility and render it inoperative."

"So, Major, are you telling me that you don't think on the battlefield? You just follow orders even if they result in the loss of the primary objective?"

Beauregard stopped and looked down at the man in the expensive three-piece suit. "Bardon said nothing about data. He wants the facility shut down."

"I'm sure he does. But the data is ultimately what's important. If we can get the data *and* shut down the facility, then that's going above and beyond to get rid of this evil."

The major tilted his chin up and his eyes took on a far away look. In a moment, he looked back at Mostyn. "I'll have to talk to Bardon."

"No, you don't. You're in the field. The situation demands an immediate response. It's up to you to make the command decision."

The major smiled. "Have you always been a cowboy?"

"Giddyap."

———

Over four hundred and fifty miles away, Congresswoman Diane Steinberg was on the telephone.

"I understand, Mr. van Dyne, but my chief of staff was hit by a car yesterday. She's in the hospital..." Steinberg listened to the voice on the other end of the line. "Yes, Mr. van Dyne. This has top priority."

She heard the word "Good", and then the dial tone. She cradled the receiver.

Steinberg hated the man. He was, however, not one to be crossed. A friend of hers had a brilliant career cut short due to a scandal hitting the papers. All lies, but in politics even the hint of possible wrongdoing was frequently enough to end a career. She was in her twenty-third year serving in the House. She had no desire to retire or resign, and once you were in bed with van Dyne there was no getting out. And if you did try to leave, the consequences were worse than a bad divorce.

Van Dyne wanted this Bardon person stopped. How was she going to do that. Miriam handled these things for her and now she was in the hospital with a broken leg and possible internal injuries.

Steinberg picked up the phone and dialed a number. "Hi, John. Diane Steinberg. ... Glad you recognized my voice. Hope you didn't cringe. ... You're too kind. Say, I have a question. Do you know anything about an Office of Unidentified Phenomena? ... Never heard of it? The agency is supposed to be in your department. ... I see. Ever hear of a Dr. Rafe Bardon? ... I see. I guess someone's trying to create some excitement. ... What do I mean? Supposedly, this agency is spying on prominent American citizens right here in the US. ... I'm sorry you can't help, too. Bye."

She cradled the receiver, and leaned back in her chair. She closed her eyes and spoke her thoughts out loud. "If I can't get what I want by means of frontal assault, maybe I can get what I want by going through the back door."

Steinberg sat up and picked up the phone. Her finger punched buttons for the phone number of a reporter she knew. A young woman always eager to expose government corruption.

16

On the other side of the District of Columbia, Dr. Rafe Bardon cradled the receiver of his phone. His conversation with the Undersecretary of Homeland Security for Intelligence and Analysis, the man who was technically his boss, had not gone well.

Congresswoman Steinberg and now a reporter were becoming increasingly bold in their demands for information. And Bardon knew his boss, nominal though he may be, didn't want to chance the possibility of publicity. Which meant an assault on the Vautier mansion, even though in a somewhat remote area of Appalachia, was fast becoming a non-option.

Bardon puffed on his pipe. He looked over at the statue of Cthulhu, carved out of the strange green stone that made the image seem alive. He chuckled. It was, however, mirthless.

His eyes shifted to the corner of the room near the statue. It didn't look right. It didn't follow the pattern of Euclidean geometry. That is to say, it wasn't *normal*. At least normal as defined by everyday standards. By common building standards. He made a mental note to run the computer program which would renew the talisman.

"If only the likes of the Congresswoman and Van Dyne knew about you and the others," Bardon murmured. "Then they'd know how truly insignificant this little planet is in the vast expanse of not only the universe and this dimension, but how insignificant even this universe is in the complexity of the multiverse. We are less than the ants on the sidewalk that we so blithely crush out of existence on a pleasant summer's day."

He puffed on his pipe and redirected his attention from the corner of his room that was slowly disintegrating into... Well, Bardon didn't exactly know. Nor did he wish to find out. He decided to jot himself an actual note to run the program, and, when pen left paper, leaned back in his chair.

"Steinberg and van Dyne's lust for power makes as much sense as the tadpole in a shrinking mud puddle thinking the world is his oyster," he said to the empty room.

He sat up and set his pipe on the desk. Mostyn will get his wish, he thought. But first he had to talk with Dr. Kemper and Ms. Dubreuil.

———

Mostyn and Beauregard were surveying the area around the Vautier mansion in a autogyro. The pilot was making lazy circles, while the two men planned the attack on the place that was probably a secret Van Dyne facility.

"We have about forty minutes of daylight left," the pilot said.

"Head back to the airport," Beauregard replied. To Mostyn, he said, "You sure this is going to work?"

Mostyn shrugged. "About as sure as my car starting in the morning."

"So the answer is, probably."

"You got it, Major."

The airport wasn't far, even so, at the slow speed of the autogyro, twenty minutes passed before they landed. During that time Mostyn phoned Jones and told him to get everyone to Pine Bluff, and that he'd meet them at the Branch Water Bar. Waiting for them when they landed was Beauregard's car and driver.

"Come on, Mostyn. I'll take you to Pine Bluff."

Mostyn got in the car and on the way to the hamlet, he got a call from Bardon.

"Pierce, my boy, van Dyne is working the bureaucracy angle to shut down our operation. I need you to go in as quietly as possible and neutralize the site. Is the major with you?"

"Yes, sir. We're in his car."

"Put the phone on speaker."

Mostyn tapped a virtual button. "You're on, sir."

"Major Beauregard? Rafe Bardon here."

"Hello, sir."

"There are problems on the Washington end. We can't risk you going in. People are watching and your team is too high profile. You will be back-up to Mostyn. I'm sending three more agents to you, Pierce. They should be there in about an hour. How you neutralize the Vautier mansion is up to you, but keep it as quiet as possible."

"Yes, sir," Mostyn said. "Understand, sir."

"Good. Very good. Best of luck to both of you."

Mostyn and Beauregard thanked Bardon for his well wishes and the call ended.

Beauregard laughed. "Your plan is now official."

"Van Dyne must really have a boatload of connections to stir up the pot to that degree."

"Probably does. It's all politics these days. Everyone

greasing a palm." The major shook his head. "Politics. You can't live with it and can't live without it."

The major's car drove into Pine Bluff and parked near the bar.

"Here you go, Mostyn. I'll be back with my men and we'll provide backup should you need it."

"Thanks, Beau."

They shook hands and Mostyn exited the vehicle. He watched the major's car drive off, and when the taillights disappeared from view he entered the bar.

Aside from his team, Mostyn counted fifteen locals. Not bad, he thought, for a weeknight. He walked over to the table his team had claimed. He was glad to see Dotty and Helene. They weren't sitting next to each other, but they weren't trying to kill each other either. He took a seat between Ramsey and Baker. A waitress appeared and he ordered a club soda. When she left, Mostyn began talking.

"Bardon has given the go ahead for us to neutralize Van Dyne's operations at the Vautier mansion. Beauregard's unit will provide back up."

"Why the change?" Jones asked.

"Politics, apparently," Mostyn replied. "Somebody's started sniffing around and Bardon's worried Beauregard's operation would be too big of a splash. He's sending us three more agents."

The conversation paused while Mostyn got his drink. When the server left, Dotty asked, "So who's actually going in?"

"Ramsey will use the drones to create a diversion and provide on the ground surveillance. Baker and Gerstner, you can assist. Jones, myself, and the three other agents will enter through the cave."

"And what will Dotty and I do, Mostyn Pierce?" Helene asked.

"I want you two to sit this one out."

"Nothing doing, Mostyn," Dotty said. "With Penn off examining the body of the Lessing Vampire, you need someone with knowledge of forensics and that's me. I need to go along."

"And I can get all of us into the facility without being seen," Helene said.

"She has a point, Mostyn," Dotty said. "A big point. How much time do you want to waste traipsing through the forest? What's that famous quote about winning battles?"

Jones let out a laugh. "Confederate General Nathan B. Forrest. Get there first and with the most men. I agree, Boss. The women make sense."

Mostyn looked at Dotty, then Helene, and then back to Dotty.

"We're okay, Mostyn," Dotty said. "Bardon talked to us. Did his astral projection thing."

A skeptical look fixed itself on Mostyn's face.

"Seriously. We're okay," Dotty repeated.

He switched his gaze to Helene.

"We are ready for this mission, Mostyn Pierce."

"All right, then, you two will come along."

Helene looked like a kid who'd been told to take one of everything from the candy store.

"Now that we got that out of the way," Baker began, "I think you need me along. I can shoot pictures and I can shoot a gun. And on this operation you just might need both."

Before Mostyn could answer, Gerstner spoke up. "And since this van Dyne is basing his creatures on legends, I might be very helpful in identifying the source of those things he's made and their potential weaknesses."

Mostyn ran his fingers over his crewcut. "Okay, okay. You two can join, as well."

Jones let out a laugh. "The Magnificent Seven and the farmers."

Mostyn caste a glance in Jones's direction. "Only the farmers won that one. Let's hope this story ends better."

―――――

The time was just before one in the morning. Some five thousand feet above the Vautier mansion a reconnaissance airship hovered, feeding video and infrared images to Mostyn and his team. By each of the two entrance roads, Beauregard had a team hidden amongst the trees. A third team was at a nearby airfield on board a helicopter.

Mostyn looked over his people. He knew one of the three special agents Bardon had sent him: Kymbra NicAskill. The other two, Caleb Lillibridge and Jim Hernandez, Mostyn knew their names and reputations, he just hadn't worked with them before.

The crescent moon was in the western sky. No clouds obscured the stars. The team was on the road by the boulder that marked where they needed to enter the woods for the shortest route to the cave entrance.

They were dressed in black jumpsuits, black gloves, black boots, and wore black helmets with face visors and tactical lights. The visors provided night vision capability, as well as display screens for information. Each team member also had a headset for audio and verbal communication.

The weapons they carried were silenced semi-automatic pistols and a backup gun of their choice; silenced submachine guns, except for Jones, who opted for a shotgun; combat knife; and grenades: one thermite, three smoke, and three stun.

"Listen up, people," Mostyn began. "To repeat. Helene and I will proceed to the cave entrance in a dematerialized state. We will see what the situation is, and if we can easily access the cave she will bring the rest of you. Once we are all at the cave entrance, we will enter, and neutralize the place."

Mostyn turned to Ramsey. "Send the drones in and let's see what they tell us."

The special agents and Helene crowded around Ramsey's screen to see what the little machines revealed about the path and defenses.

Jones said, "Looks the same. Cameras, laser tripwires for alarms, and nature's pitfalls."

"That it does, Jones," Mostyn replied.

The drones flew through the forest and then abruptly emerged into a small clearing at the base of a hill. Ramsey sent a number of drones up the steep hillside until the Vautier mansion came into view.

"The cave entrance should be somewhere here," Ramsey said, as he directed the drones into a search pattern.

The forest clearing had some grasses and bushes. The base of the hillside was dominated by two large trees, between which were tall bushes.

Ramsey directed several drones to fly through the bushes.

"Hot damn!" Jones exclaimed, for on the other side of the bushes was an opening about five feet by four feet with chain link fencing covering it.

"Now we know what to look for and what we need to do to enter," Mostyn said.

"Entering will be easy, Mostyn Pierce," Helene said, "but what is on the other side?"

"Easy to find out," Ramsey replied. He directed several drones to fly through the chain link fence. Their little lights provided scanty illumination in the darkness of the tunnel.

"Aha!" Ramsey exclaimed, and pointed to the screen. "The heat sensors are picking up two large objects." He fiddled with a couple virtual dials, and then pointed to the screen again. "There. And there. Looks like those three-headed dogs they're so fond of."

"Good work, Ramsey," Mostyn said. "How far in are they?"

"Looks like about eighty feet."

"Thanks." To Helene, Mostyn said, "Ready to go?"

"Yes, Mostyn Pierce."

"Then let's go." He pulled back the bolt to cock the submachine gun, and disappeared, along with Helene Dubreuil.

17

DEMATERIALIZED, Mostyn and Helene had no trouble making their way to the cave entrance. A cloud of atoms floating through the forest. They rematerialized in the small clearing. Helene sent her thoughts to Mostyn.

Do you want to wait here while I get the others, or should we go inside?

Mostyn pondered the situation for a moment, and sent his thoughts to her. *Something about this doesn't seem right. Those trees look fake.*

Do you mean they are not real? she thought back.

More or less. They don't look right. The bark isn't quite normal. The leaves don't look like tree leaves. The way the branches are shaped doesn't look like any natural tree shape I'm familiar with.

Mostyn took out his knife and walked up to the tree to the right of the cave opening. He touched the bark. No, not right. He took off his glove, and touched again. It felt almost... Slimy, Mostyn thought.

He slipped his glove back on and cut into the bark with his knife. All hell broke loose. The branches began thrashing him and coiling about him like tentacles. He slashed at the tree limbs with his knife and then vanished.

In his now dematerialize state, he easily escaped from the tree's clutches and returned to Helene's side, where she rematerialized him.

The tree was once again still. The only movement being that of a few of the leaves stirring in the light breeze.

"I guess that takes GMO plant material to a whole new level," Mostyn said.

"Oh, Mostyn Pierce, you are making a joke!"

"Yeah, right."

"I will take care of the tree," Helene said.

She went still, focused on the thing, and then it vanished. A moment later only its roots rematerialized and they were sticking out of the hillside.

"Let's hope van Dyne doesn't get wind of you," Mostyn said, while pointing to the other tree.

In a moment, it too was buried in the hillside.

"Now do we enter the cave, Mostyn Pierce?"

"You enter and see if there are any cameras."

Helene vanished, and Mostyn scanned the hillside. He saw nothing to indicate any other sentinels. Perhaps the big wigs at Van Dyne Corp figured the trees were enough.

Mostyn pushed his way through the bushes in front of the cave opening and examined where the chain link fence met the cave wall, looking for any indication the fence was wired. While doing so, Helene's thoughts entered his mind.

There are two cameras about ten or fifteen feet inside the cave entrance, one on either side. What do you want to do about them?

Mostyn sent back his thoughts. *Leave them for the moment and get the others. Bring a cutter for the fence, too.*

I'll be back, my love.

Be careful, Mostyn thought back.

Once again he looked over the cave entrance, and when he was satisfied there wasn't anything else to see, turned and looked at the trees on the edge of the clearing. He didn't see any surveillance devices, but that didn't mean there weren't any. In this day of miniaturization, cameras were the size of a quarter or smaller. Drones looked like bugs. For all he knew, the Van Dyne security team was watching him right now. And they probably were. At least he'd have to assume they were, until he knew otherwise.

He walked over to the tree line and hunkered down by a tree, across from the cave entrance, and waited for Helene's return. It didn't take long. Before he knew it, materializing there before him, were Jones, Baker, and Kemper.

Mostyn signaled to them to join him. Helene waved to him, and was gone.

"What's the story?" Jones asked.

"The two trees by the entrance?" Mostyn said.

"Yes. Helene said something about them being alive?"

Mostyn pointed. "See those roots? That's them. They were some kind of GMO creation of Van Dyne's. The one attacked me. The limbs were like tentacles."

"Holy shit," Dotty said. "This is getting surreal."

"I would have liked to have gotten pictures of them," Baker said.

Helene returned with Dr. Gerstner and the three agents, and asked, "Now what do we do, Mostyn Pierce?"

He held up a finger. "To finish answering your question, Jones," Mostyn said, "there's a chain link fence behind those bushes. About ten feet into the cave are surveillance cameras, and beyond them are the Cerberus creatures. A pair of them."

"And God knows what else," Jones replied.

Mostyn nodded. "Exactly. Lillibridge and Hernandez, take the cutters and make a hole for us in the fence. Helene, go in now and take out the cameras. Hopefully, the Van Dyne monsters won't respond too quickly."

Helene disappeared and the two agents went to the cave entrance to work on the fence. In a minute, Lillibridge was motioning for the team to advance. One by one they slipped through the bushes and the hole in the fence.

Inside the cave entrance, Helene reappeared.

"The cameras are no longer in service. I have also destroyed the three-headed dogs. The cave is clear. We should hurry, Mostyn Pierce."

Mostyn said, "You heard the lady. What are you waiting for?"

With Mostyn and Jones in the lead, and NicAskill the rear guard, the team moved deeper into the cave. The lights mounted on their helmets cast bouncing beams of brilliant white light, which caused the cave walls to glisten.

"A wet cave," Gerstner said.

"As opposed to what, a dry cave?" Hernandez asked.

"Precisely," Gerstner replied.

Baker added, "A dry cave is one which has stopped forming. A wet cave is in the process of forming and developing."

Gerstner continued, "The water carving out the soft rock, forming the tunnels, and also things like this." He stopped a moment to gaze at the ribbon-patterned rock.

"And the more familiar stalactites and stalagmites," Baker said.

"Are you guys cave specialists?" Lillibridge asked.

"Amateur spelunkers," Gerstner and Baker replied in unison, looked at each other, and let out a laugh.

"Pay attention back there," Mostyn said in a stage whisper.

The team came to the curve where the Cerberus monsters had been detected by Ramsey's drones. The only thing visible were two butts, with tails, sticking out of the rock.

"Damn," Kemper said. "You have to teach me that."

"I will, my sister," Helene replied.

"I'm…" Kemper paused, and then said, "Thanks, Helene."

The cave floor began to angle up. A branch split off to the left and appeared to descend deeper into the earth.

Mostyn spoke. "Ramsey, can you send some drones in here. I'd like an idea as to where these two branches terminate."

"Sure, Mostyn. They'll be there in a jiffy."

"Dale, do you guys see anything?"

"Your eye in the sky reports minimal activity at the moment. The most active area seems to be the second floor of the house. Nothing in your immediate neighborhood."

"Thanks," Mostyn replied.

A cloud of drones, each one about the size of a praying mantis, flew into view. Traveling along the ceiling of the cave, they split into two groups: one taking the high road, and the other taking the low road. And in a few seconds, Ramsey's voice sounded in the team's ears.

"The upper path ends in a large and what looks to be a heavy door. Just a minute." There was a brief pause, before Ramsey continued. "And it looks like you have visitors coming from the lower level." Another pause, and then, "Oh, God! Get out! Get out!"

18

MOSTYN GAVE the signal to fall back, and the team made for the cave entrance, Ramsey's drones leading the way. Mostyn and Jones hung back a bit and tossed two smoke grenades into the descending cave branch.

"Hopefully that slows them down," Jones said.

"Hopefully." Mostyn indicated Jones should head for the cave entrance.

"No heroics, Boss."

Mostyn nodded, and they both began trotting towards the entrance. Behind them they heard a chorus of deep-throated growls and short, sharp barks.

"Oh, shit," Jones said, "I don't think Plan A is working."

"Apparently not," Mostyn replied.

They stopped, turned, and saw a pack of three-headed dogs running their way. Mostyn pulled the trigger on his submachine gun. Jones pulled the trigger on his shotgun, pumped in a new round, and pulled the trigger again. Repeating the process faster than it takes to turn around. In mere moments, a dozen giant carcasses littered the cave floor. The two agents reloaded their weapons.

The rest of the team arrived. Mostyn looked at them and asked what they were doing there.

"We heard gunfire," Lillibridge said, "and came to help."

NicAskill took one look and said, "Just like in New Jersey."

Lillibridge yelled, "Look!"

Following his pointing finger, the team saw four creatures coming towards them. They had four arms and four legs attached to a body that looked like a freezer chest. On each end of the body was a head on a longish neck.

Not waiting for orders, NicAskill opened fire, followed by Lillibridge and Hernandez. The four creatures fell in a heap, but behind them were more and they fired back.

Hernandez wasn't quick enough and took several bullets. The rest of the team hit the cave floor. Mostyn and Jones each tossed a stun grenade. The flash-bang caused momentary confusion amongst the things, enough for Kemper and Baker to pop up and empty their submachine guns into the monstrosities.

Several of the bizarre beings fell, but more of the things kept coming. NicAskill, Lillibridge, and Jones fired into the oncoming horde. Blood and bone spray covered the cave passage, and monstrosity after monstrosity dropped dead to the floor. When the three agents ran out of ammunition, Mostyn, Kemper, and Baker took their place. When they, too, had emptied the magazines for their weapons, none of the Van Dyne laboratory creations were standing. A couple dozen of the large, bullet-riddled, pulpy bodies covered the cave floor.

"Good God," Kemper said. "What else does he have?"

"These things aren't from any mythology," Gerstner said, examining one of the bodies. "They are pure imagination."

"A sick and twisted imagination," NicAskill added, as she and Lillibridge knelt by Hernandez.

"Is he...?" Mostyn let the question hang.

NicAskill shook her head. Lillibridge, with Jones's help, moved Hernandez's body over to the side of the cave tunnel.

Mostyn took a look over the battlefield. "Where's Helene?"

Shrugs and a few "I don't know"s answered his question.

Mostyn keyed his mic. "Helene, respond if you can hear me."

"Anything?" Kemper asked.

He shook his head. "Nothing. Where the hell is she?" He closed his eyes, formed a picture of her in his mind, and thought, *Where are you?*

In his mind, he heard her say, *I am on the other side of the door. It is an entrance to a cellar. We need to be here.*

Okay, he thought back. *Come back here.*

Yes, my husband.

"Well?" Dotty asked.

"She followed the cave passage to the door that Ramsey mentioned and passed through into a cellar."

"She just left us...?" NicAskill didn't get to finish her statement because Helene materialized next to Dotty.

"There are very interesting things in the cellar I visited," Helene said.

"You just abandoned us?" NicAskill said, her hands on her hips.

"Oh, no. I dematerialized and went behind the creatures and helped you." She pointed. "See?"

Barely visible in the cave walls, floor, and ceiling were the soles of a couple dozen feet.

NicAskill didn't say anything. She walked over to the cave wall and touched one of the soles. The flesh gave as her finger poked it. Only then did she mutter, "Well, I'll be damned."

Mostyn asked, "Can you dematerialize all of us together so we can check out the cellar?"

"I don't think so, Mostyn Pierce. This many people is difficult to manage."

"Listen up," Mostyn began. "Jones, Lillibridge, NicAskill, and myself will go with Helene—"

Kemper interrupted. "Oh, no you don't, Mostyn. No. I'm taking NicAskill's place."

"Wait one minute," NicAskill began, but didn't get to finish.

A scream rent the air, followed by the sound of automatic weapons fire. Charging down the cave tunnel were more of the Cerberus-like monsters, followed by several two-headed ogre-like creatures.

Jones, who had been on point watching for more monsters, returned fire with his shotgun.

The team dropped to the cave floor and returned fire. When his shotgun was empty, Jones tossed a stun grenade, and began shooting his pistol.

One of the three-headed dogs got by Jones and launched itself at Lillibridge, who had stood up to get a better angle of fire after the flash-bang of the stun grenade. All three hundred pounds of the beast landed on the special agent, three sets of jaws biting him. Then the monster was gone. Only a tail reappeared hanging from the ceiling.

Two of the ogre things charged into the team. A third creature had Jones pushed up against the cave wall.

A stream of lead from NicAskill's submachine gun stopped one of the two-headed creatures. The other one disappeared. The third creature had a hand around Jones's throat and had lifted him off the ground. Suddenly the creature roared, Jones dropped, and the thing staggered back: its entrails falling to the cave floor. Baker fired his submachine gun at it, and the monster shook with the impact of the bullets and fell backwards onto the floor. Jones wiped his knife off on the thing's leg.

"How many of these things have they created?" Gerstner asked.

"Too goddamn many," Dotty replied.

Mostyn keyed his mic. "Beau, it's time for you guys to move in."

Dale's voice sounded in their ears. "This is Sky Command. We're detecting lots of activity now."

"What kind of activity?" Mostyn asked.

Beauregard's voice. "Two armored cars just came out of the southeast drive, like the proverbial bats out of hell. I've dispatched pursuit vehicles."

Dale's voice. "A helicopter has just taken off. And now there's smoke. It looks like they've torched the place."

Mostyn spoke. "Beau, get your people in there and try to put the fire out."

"Copy, Mostyn. On our way."

To his team, Mostyn said, "Looks like they're abandoning ship. As you heard, they have set fire to the mansion. We need to act quickly. Helene, Jones, Dotty, you're with me. We're going to check out the cellar before it's too late. The rest of you, get out of here. Lillibridge?"

"He's lost blood and I think he has broken bones," NicAskill replied. "We'll get him out."

"Good," Mostyn said. He turned to Helene, and said, "Dematerialize us."

19

THE CELLAR LOOKED MORE like a lab than a place where grandma stored her pickles and preserves. The walls were white and the room was brightly lit. There were three rows of metal shelving filled with glass containers. In each container was a tiny monstrosity, and there had to be hundreds of them. Tubes and wires ran from the containers to junction boxes and from the junction boxes to wall outlets.

Dotty peered closely at one container. "This one's going to be a three-headed dog."

Jones looked at another. "This one has two heads."

"This is the nursery from hell," Dotty said.

"This one is a worm," Helene said. "We have not seen any worms."

"Not yet," Mostyn replied. "And I'm guessing it's a snake and we probably don't want to meet it."

"We need to take some of these with us," Dotty said. "The proof is in the pudding and here's the pudding."

Mostyn looked at a container with its tubes and wires. "Can these be disconnected?"

"They can," Dotty replied. "Although the creatures will probably die."

Mostyn nodded. "But they shouldn't deteriorate before we get them to a government lab. Right?"

Dotty shrugged. "Probably not."

"Jones, do you think we can get this door open?" Mostyn asked.

He looked over the heavy metal door, then shrugged. "We could if we had tools. Or we could use the thermite grenades."

Mostyn shook his head. "Don't want to use the thermite. Everyone grab a container."

When everyone had a container in their arms, Mostyn gave the order for Helene to dematerialize them

The four OUP operatives vanished and then reappeared on the other side of the cellar door.

"Okay, people," Mostyn said, "let's get the hell out of here."

Down the cave they walked at a brisk pace. When they reached the place where the branch that descended deeper into the earth split off, Mostyn set down his container, pulled the submachine gun around from his back, slipped the sling off his shoulder, and listened intently at the opening.

After a few moments, he waved the rest of his team on. He lingered to make sure Van Dyne didn't have any stragglers coming late to the party. When he was satisfied all was going to remain quiet, he slipped the sling over his head, and put the submachine gun behind him. He picked up the container, and caught up with the rest of his team.

"I think Van Dyne's exhausted his supply of uglies," Mostyn said.

The hill above them shook.

"What's happening?" Helene asked.

"Off hand," Jones said, "I think they're blowing up the place."

"Makes sense," Mostyn added. "Too much evidence could survive a fire."

A dull thud reached their ears, and the cave shook.

"That one was closer to home," Mostyn said. "Let's double time it."

They ran towards the cave entrance.

"I still think this is too easy," Jones said.

"Don't jinx it," Dotty replied.

Coming up to the bend in the cave that signaled they were near the entrance, they heard a dull thud, followed by a sound like thunder, and then felt the cave shudder. Kemper and Jones stumbled, but stayed on their feet. From behind, everyone felt a rush of wind.

"What is that?" Helene said.

Mostyn turned, and his helmet lamps picked up two glowing eyes. From their size and their distance apart, he guessed the head to be huge. He dropped his jar, which broke on the stone floor, and pulled his submachine gun around. Everyone else turned and the combined beams of light revealed the head of a giant serpent. A head which almost filled the cave tunnel.

Mostyn opened fire. The snake opened its mouth, scooped up the special agent, and closed its jaws.

20

JONES AND KEMPER OPENED FIRE, their glass jars lying broken on the floor where they'd dropped them. The two streams of bullets poured into the snake's head, destroying the thing's eyes.

The giant reptile's tongue flicked out of the huge mouth. It hit Helene and knocked her into the cave wall. She collapsed to the floor.

Jones and Kemper slammed new magazines into their weapons. From inside the creature, they heard gunfire and then silence.

The mouth opened revealing two large fangs. Jones and Kemper fired into the gaping orifice before them.

"The roof of the mouth to get its brain," Dotty yelled.

Jones adjusted his aim. The creature began writhing. Its mouth opening and closing. It bashed its head into the cave wall and lay still.

"We've got to get Mostyn!" Dotty yelled. "Your knife, Jones!"

They began slashing at the thing.

"We're never going to get through these scales," Jones said.

"We have to get him out. He'll suffocate in there."

"Can we get under it?" Jones asked. "The underside should be easier."

"I don't see how. It's too big. Practically fills the cave." Dotty hung her head. "This is never going to work." Suddenly her head shot up. "The thermite grenades. We'll burn a hole in the son of a bitch."

"Whoa, Dot. They burn too hot. You might burn Mostyn."

Dotty's face was mere inches from Jones's. "He's dying! Give me your goddamn grenade."

Jones was too slow and Dotty grabbed the thing off his belt. With her knife she carved a small hole in the snake, pulled the pin, and shoved the grenade into the hole.

She and Jones ran back from the creature. A brilliant flame shot out. The smell of burnt flesh filled the cave. After half a minute, there was a large crater in the snake. Dotty ran up to the thing and checked the hole.

"Not big enough," she said, grabbed her own grenade, pulled the pin, and shoved it into the crater. She ran back to Jones. In four seconds a brilliant white flame shot into the air. Burnt flesh scented the damp cave air. And thirty seconds later the flame was gone.

She and Jones ran over to the creature and began digging through the cooked and burnt flesh with their knives.

"He can't be in too far," she said. "The snake didn't have time to get him down its gullet."

"Hey! What's this?" Jones asked.

"The thing's throat! We can do it! Just follow until we get to Mostyn."

They continued carving their way through the snake's flesh, like surgeons doing emergency surgery. "Come on, come on." Dotty kept muttering under her breath.

"A boot!" Jones yelled.

"Here's the other one!" Dotty said. "Pull, Jones!"

The agents grabbed Mostyn's boots, and pulled. Stopped a moment, and pulled again. Out he popped like a baby being born. He was covered with slime and blood and burnt snake flesh.

"Oh, God, he's not breathing." Dotty started giving him mouth-to-mouth resuscitation, and Jones began pushing on his chest. After a moment, Mostyn gasped, then coughed. His eyes fluttered open.

"He's alive!" Dotty said. "Oh, God, Mostyn, I thought we'd lost you."

"Lose Mostyn? That'd be like losing Superman," Jones quipped.

Mostyn lifted his head, shook it, and groaned. Dotty hugged and kissed him.

"Is it getting hot in here?" Jones asked.

"The fire," Kemper said. "Must be getting closer. We have to get out of here."

Jones scooped up Mostyn, said, "I got him. You see to Helene," and made for the cave entrance.

Smoke was beginning to seep around the giant snake carcass. Dotty looked at Helene lying on the cave floor.

"I could just leave you here, couldn't I? Leave you, and have Mostyn all to myself. Just like it was before you showed up. Just tell them I couldn't wake you, and the smoke drove me off."

She stood there looking at the K'n-yanian. For how long she didn't know, although it probably wasn't more than a few seconds. Then she turned and picked up the specimens and headed for the tunnel entrance.

After a dozen steps Dotty Kemper stopped. She turned around and looked at Helene. The smoke was beginning to get thick in the cave. She set down the embryos, and ran to

Helene.

Dotty shook her. "Come on, Helene, wake up." When there was no response, she took the K'n-yanian's canteen and emptied the water on her head. Helene sputtered and opened her eyes.

"Come on. We have to leave, before we're nothing more than smoked long pig."

"Long pig? What's that?"

"Later."

Dotty helped Helene to stand up. "Can you walk?"

"I, I think so," Helene answered. She took a few tentative steps, and nodded.

They made for the cave entrance, retrieved the embryos of the monsters, and continued walking until they reached the fence. NicAskill was waiting for them.

"Come on!" NicAskill said. "The cave is starting to fill with smoke."

They pushed through the fence opening and came into the clearing, where Jones, Mostyn, and Gerstner were waiting.

"Is everyone accounted for?" Mostyn asked.

NicAskill replied, "We couldn't retrieve Hernandez's body." She looked over at the smoke coming out of the cave entrance. "Maybe after the fire. Some of the Special Forces guys took Lillibridge to the hospital. Gerstner and I opted to wait for you."

Mostyn smiled. "Thanks, Kymbra. Doctor."

Gerstner gave him a nod.

Mostyn turned and looked at Dotty. "Did you save the specimens?"

"I did," Dotty replied.

"Good." Relief was written all over Mostyn's face. "We have to get them to a lab."

"Penn ought to have lots of fun," Dotty said. "Too bad I'm

only going to have charred remains to examine." She paused, then asked, "How are you?"

"Other than this slime, I think I'm okay. Thanks." He kissed her. "And thank you again, Jones."

"Don't mention it, Boss. All in a day's work."

Mostyn turned to Helene. "I heard you were knocked out. Are you okay?"

She nodded. "Yes, I think so, Mostyn Pierce."

"You might have a concussion," Dotty said. "We need to get you to a doctor. That thing slammed you pretty hard against the wall."

There was a high-pitched scream and crashing into the clearing was a giant squid on six legs, like those of an ant. One of the two long tentacles wrapped itself around Jones, yanking him back towards a viciously snapping beak.

NicAskill opened fire with her submachine gun. A stream of lead poured into the creature, severing several of the shorter tentacles and turning the beak into a bloody, pulpy mess.

The other long tentacle reached out and swept NicAskill off her feet. Kemper jumped up, ran to the side of the creature and opened fire with her submachine gun, directing the stream of bullets to just behind the eye. The monster let out a high-pitched scream and pitched forward onto the ground. It shuddered and was still.

Kemper was all smiles. "I guess I won't have only charred remains to examine."

Mostyn walked over to the thing. "Good shooting, Dot. How did you know what to aim for?"

"I may be a forensic anthropologist, but working for the OUP has taught me that Van Dyne doesn't even begin to have a monopoly on the weird."

Mostyn laughed. "Ain't that the truth."

Dotty added, "Besides, in biology class I learned that the squid's brain is behind where the eyes are."

"Thank God for good old biology," Mostyn said. He turned to Helene. "You feel well enough? Do you think you can do your thing and get us back to the road?"

Helene sent her thoughts to him. *Of course, my husband.* And with that, she, Mostyn, and Dotty disappeared.

EPILOGUE

DR. RAFE BARDON sat behind his desk, puffing on his pipe. Before him, sitting in identical chocolate leather tub chairs, were Pierce Mostyn, Dotty Kemper, and Helene Dubreuil.

Bardon set his pipe down. "The Vautier mansion is a total ruin. We have a forensics team going through the wreckage to see if anything remains that the public should not discover. Otherwise, the main thing of value we have are the specimens you retrieved. Good work, you three. In fact, your entire team was exemplary, Pierce."

"Thank you, sir. Was Beauregard able to capture any of the workers?"

"The helicopter and the armored trucks escaped. His men did round up a few of the workers, but it looks as though most escaped into the forest. Or maybe through secret tunnels. The ones we captured were low-level workers and I don't think we'll get much out of them."

"That's too bad, sir," Mostyn replied.

Bardon shrugged. "At least that facility is out of commission. And, let me repeat, your team did exemplary work. I may even make Special Agent NicAskill a regular for you."

"Are you replacing Jones?" Mostyn asked.

"Oh, no," Bardon replied. "Given the nature of your missions, I'm thinking it will be better for you to have two agents."

"I see."

"You don't seem too happy, Pierce."

"Oh, no, Dr. Bardon. No, sir. I think NicAskill will be a great addition. Very capable."

Bardon was all smiles. "Good."

"What about van Dyne, sir?" Mostyn asked.

"I got a message from him shortly after his people destroyed the mansion. In a rather bad rendition of Arnold's voice, he said he'd be back. And I do not doubt it. We have not seen the last of Valdis Damien van Dyne."

"Do we know why he was creating these creatures, sir?" Mostyn asked.

"Not really. We have not been able to access his records. They are very well protected. My guess is that they were intended for very specialized military, paramilitary, or security use. But that is just a guess. A good guess, I think, since one of his creatures seems to have been in operation in Africa. At least that's what the latest intelligence we've gathered indicates."

Mostyn nodded and had a faraway look on his face.

"What about the Congresswoman?" Dotty asked.

Bardon shrugged. "She's a politician, and consequently thinks she actually has power." He looked over at the statues of Cthulhu and Shub-Niggurath. "Of course we know differently."

"Why don't you just zap them?" Dotty said.

Bardon chuckled. "Zap them? You don't just go around *zapping* what you don't like, Dr. Kemper. These entities we occasionally utilize are powerful beings. They seek to use us as much as we try to use them. Maybe even more so. It's best if we handle things with the resources available to us on this little speck of rock we call home. There is always a quid pro quo, Dr. Kemper. Always. Do keep that in mind."

Dotty nodded.

"For now, anyway," Mostyn said, "there shouldn't be anymore sightings of chupacabras, Jersey Devils, or Lessing Vampires."

"No, there shouldn't," Bardon said, and after a pause, added, "At least of Van Dyne's manufacture."

"You mean…," Kemper began.

"Yes," Bardon said.

Kemper shook her head.

Bardon continued, "Of course, he may have other facilities creating these things."

"And probably worse things," Dotty said.

Bardon nodded. "Yes. Even worse monstrosities. So we may indeed run into his little playthings in the future." He turned to Helene. "You are awfully quiet, my dear."

Helene smiled. "I am very happy we are all here."

"Yes, indeed," Bardon said. He turned to Mostyn. "We almost lost you, Pierce."

"My sister and Jones saved him," Helene said. She smiled at Dotty and Dotty actually smiled back.

"Always glad to see teamwork in the heat of the battle," Bardon said. "Very glad." He picked up his pipe. "Well, tomorrow is another day." He stood. "Off with you now. Enjoy the afternoon."

The three left, but not before Helene bowed to the statue of Cthulhu. Bardon returned to his seat. He looked at the roiling indefiniteness that was the corner of the room near Cthulhu, its unnatural angles and lines. It was as though something was trying to break through.

He thought to himself, *Yes, indeed, Dr. Kemper, there is always a quid pro quo.*

A WORD FROM CW

I hope you enjoyed *Van Dyne's Vampires.*

If you did, please leave a review where you bought the book and on your favorite social media sites. Your review is like word of mouth advertising. And it is pure gold.

Enter my World

Enter my world. A world of terror on a cosmic scale. Just click, tap, or scan the QR code below.

Fear is the most primal of human emotions. And fear of the unknown is the most terrifying of all fears.

If you are new to the Pierce Mostyn Paranormal Investigations series, then *Van Dyne's Vampires* is an excellent entry point into the series and into my world.

In addition to my Pierce Mostyn Paranormal Investigations books, I've written short stories set in the world of the macabre and arcane. Many of which are only available to folks on my mailing list.

So just click, tap, or scan the QR code to enter my world of terror and the macabre. You will get a free copy of *The Feeder* and you'll get my monthly email of news and curated contact. Terror awaits!

CONTINUE THE ADVENTURE!

The paranormal investigations of Pierce Mostyn continue in *The Medusa Ritual*. When looking fear in the eyes is the last thing you do!

Special Agent in Charge Pierce Mostyn and his team are on assignment in Los Angeles, California. Their mission? To find a rare book of forbidden knowledge before the owner can unleash unthinkable terror upon the world.

And when a mysterious mask-wearing man, dressed in Chinese robes upends the mission and captures Mostyn's part-ner, Dr. Dotty Kemper — things take a very personal turn for Mostyn.

To rescue Dotty, Mostyn and his team follow the clues deep into the crumbling tunnel system beneath Los Angeles. In this deadly labyrinth, Mostyn is in a race against time to stop the mysterious man. But around every corner will they discover the mysterious man, Dotty, or the dreaded Gorgon herself?

The Medusa Ritual is available at your favorite online store. Check it out!

BOOKS BY CW HAWES

CW is a multi-genre author.

The books below are portals to his many exciting worlds. And no AI was used in the writing of these books. Books by a human for a human.

Pierce Mostyn Paranormal Investigations

The X-Files meets Cthulhu. Pierce Mostyn does battle with inter-dimensional monsters bent on the destruction of humanity.

Nightmare in Agate Bay
Stairway to Hell
Terror in the Shadows
Van Dyne's Vampires
The Medusa Ritual
Demons in the Dunes
Van Dyne's Zuvembies
In the Shadow of the Mountains of Madness

Justinia Wright Private Investigator Mysteries

Justinia Wright is the PI with panache. These slow burn mysteries, written in homage to Rex Stout's Nero Wolfe, are sure to satisfy your craving for intriguing puzzles, quirky characters, and wise-cracking humor.

Vampire House and Other Early Cases of Justinia Wright, PI
Festival of Death
Trio in Death-Sharp Minor
But Jesus Never Wept
The Conspiracy Game
A Nest of Spies
When Friends Must Die
Death Makes a House Call
To Right a Wrong
The Nine Deadly Dolls
Ripples on the Pond
Christmas with the Wrights
Minneapolis's Finest
Jack in the Box
Sauerkraut Days
Justinia Wright Private Investigator Omnibus Edition

Magnolia Bluff Crime Chronicles

Tense slow burn mysteries set in our favorite town in the Texas Hill Country.

Death Wears a Crimson Hat
Ten Million Ways to Die
Who Mourns Elektra?
Death by Moonlight

The Rocheport Saga

A post-apocalyptic adventure series in the style of cozy catastrophes such as *Earth Abides* and *Day of the Triffids*. Join Bill Arthur as he strives to build a new and better world on the ashes of the old.

The Morning Star
The Shining City
The Divided City
The Troubled City
By Leaps and Bounds
Freedom's Freehold
Take to the Sky

Decopunk

Alternative history adventures in a world where World War II never happened and swing is still king.

From the Files of Lady Dru Drummond
The Moscow Affair
The Golden Fleece Affair

Rand Hart Adventures
Rand Hart and the Pajama Putsch

Tales of the Macabre

For the horror lover in you.
Do One Thing For Me
Metamorphosis
What the Next Day Brings
Ancient History

Anthologies

Enjoy CW's stories in these short story collections.

The Phantom Games
Beyond the Sea
Overmorrow
Arachnapocalypse! The Anthology
Once Upon a WolfPack

Available at your favorite online retailer.

ABOUT CW HAWES

CW Hawes has written over 50 novels and shorter works of fiction. He was also an award-winning poet and had over 200 poems appear in ezines and and print.

He is a founding member of the Underground Authors and was the impetus for the highly successful Magnolia Bluff Crime Chronicles series.

After 35 years of working in county government, he retired at the beginning of 2015 and began a second career as a fictioneer. Perhaps some of some of the horrors Pierce Mostyn faces can be traced to his creator's own experiences in county government and beyond. Perhaps.

CW lives in Southern California. He enjoys reading, writing, chess and other board games, his daily morning walk, and contemplating the meaning of life while smoking his pipe. He also hasn't met a doughnut or a pizza he doesn't like, is something of a tea snob, and rocks out to Handel and Vaughan Williams.

You can get curated content and the occasional free story when you join his mailing list, and you can reach him at his website, on X, and also Facebook.

To join his mailing list, click, tap, or scan the QR code:

To visit him on his website, click, tap, or scan the QR code:

To visit him on X, click, tap, or scan the QR code:

To visit him on Facebook, click, tap, or scan the QR code: